TEXAS TRACKER

THE LAREDO SHOWDOWN

TOM CALHOUN

JOVE BOOKS, NEW YORK

THE LAREDO SHOWDOWN

A Jove Book / published by arrangement with
the author

PRINTING HISTORY
Jove edition / November 2002

Copyright © 2002 by Penguin Putnam Inc.

Visit our website at
www.penguinputnam.com

ISBN: 0-515-13404-X

A JOVE BOOK®
Jove Books are published by The Berkley Publishing Group,
a division of Penguin Putnam Inc.,
375 Hudson Street, New York, New York 10014.
JOVE and the "J" design
are trademarks belonging to Penguin Putnam Inc.

PRINTED IN THE UNITED STATES OF AMERICA

10 9 8 7 6 5 4 3 2 1

ONE

✦

ZACK COVINGTON QUICKLY loaded his last five cartridges into his Winchester .44 carbine. Poking the barrel through one of the gun ports cut into the shutters, he saw two riders bearing down on his foreman, Pedro Cruz. The little man was running for his life in a desperate effort to reach the safety of the ranch house. Lying dead in the dirt behind Pedro were three other ranch hands who had been caught by surprise at the sudden appearance of the raiders. Before they could react, they had been gunned down where they stood. Only Pedro had managed to get to his gun, hanging on a corner post of the corral. Small in size, but not lacking in courage, Pedro had shot two of the attackers dead and wounded a third before making his break for the house.

Zack felt the kick of the .44-caliber rifle as his first shot knocked one of the riders out of the saddle, sending him tumbling in the dirt. Levering another round, Covington sighted in on the other man, with the wide-brimmed sombrero. The Winchester bucked again as the shot found its mark. The front of the Mexican rider's shirt exploded with a mixture of dust and blood as the bullet tore through his chest. His head went back and he rolled off the back of his horse, his body bouncing twice along the ground before coming to rest in a heap thirty feet from the front of the house.

"Martha! Get the door. Let Pedro in, then bar it back, quick!"

Covington's wife, Martha, set her rifle aside and hurried to the door. Removing the heavy oak crossbar, she peeked out through a small hole. She waited until Pedro had reached the front steps, then quickly opened the door wide. As soon as the man dived into the room, she slammed the door shut and hoisted the oak bar back in place. Kneeling down next to Cruz, who was breathing heavily, she placed her hand on his shoulder.

"Are you hit, Pedro?"

"No, *señora*. I will be fine in a moment. Thank you."

Without another word, Martha rose, went back to her position at one of the windows, and began firing out of one of the gun ports. Pedro crawled up onto his knees, wiping the sweat and dirt from his face with the sleeve of his shirt, and looked around the room. Sixteen-year-old Charlie Covington was firing away at one of the windows, while the other two Covington children, fourteen-year-old Debbie and her ten-year-old brother, Thomas, hid behind the cookstove, holding on to each other tightly. Across the room, near the fireplace, was the body of Antonio Valdez, one of the *vaqueros* Pedro had sent up to the house just before the attack. Mrs. Covington had placed a fine lace kerchief over the dead man's face. Blood stained the floor from the hole in the side of his head.

Clambering to his feet, Pedro grabbed up the rifle lying next to the dead man and moved to the window next to Zack Covington. As he looked out across the yard, he saw the bodies of eight men littering the ground. Beyond the corral were another thirty to forty riders. Some began to dismount, and working their way to the left and right of the house, took up firing positions behind whatever cover they could find. Once in position, the men began to fire a lethal barrage of hot lead into the house from all sides. The defenders of the house all dropped to the floor as bullets splintered wood and shattered windows, lamps, dishes, and pictures on the walls. Young Debbie tried to console her brother as he began to cry.

Pedro looked over to his longtime friend and boss. Zack Covington's eyes told it all. They had no chance. They were running out of ammunition and there were too many gunmen. It was just a matter of time before they would set the house ablaze to drive the defenders out. The shooting suddenly stopped. Covington eased himself up to a position where he could see out into the yard.

A single rider approached and stopped midway between the ranch house and the corral. He was dark-complexioned, and had shoulder-length black hair and a headband. He wore no shirt, only a cowhide vest with silver conchos, and had tan leather pants. Desert boots covered the lower part of his legs. The horse was a paint with a Spanish spade bit in his mouth. The man's saddle was Mexican. The horse blanket, Navajo. Zack felt a chill run the length of his spine as he suddenly realized who he was fighting.

"In the house! We will give you five minutes to come out. If you do not—we burn the house. You have no chance. You are few, while we are many. Come out with your hands in the air. There is no need for you to die. You have five minutes."

The rider wheeled his horse about and rode back to the corner of the barn. Covington slumped down to the floor and leaned back against the bullet-riddled wall.

"Comancheros," he sighed.

For a moment, his eyes met Martha's. They both looked at their children. He could see the fear in his wife's eyes. The fear of knowing what could happen to them if they fell into the hands of these godforsaken men. Moving along the floor to the stove, Martha clutched her two youngest children to her. Her eyes were filling with tears. She too knew they had no chance of escape.

"My God, Zack. Comancheros! I thought the Rangers and Colonel MacKenzie's soldiers had put an end to the Comancheros. What are they doing here now? There hasn't been a raid reported in years. What are we going to do, Zack? God, what are we going to do?"

"I don't know, Martha."

Zack Covington's hands began to tremble, not because he was scared, but because of what he was thinking. These men were killers and rapists, men of the lowest kind. He would rather see his family dead than subjected to the torture and terror these men would put them through. But how did a man put a gun to the head of a wife of thirty years and the mother of his children? How could a man look his children in the eyes, then shoot each one of them dead? The very thought of doing such a thing made him shake all over. He was a hard man, but not that hard. He knew he could never do that. He knew he couldn't save them all. But there was one way he might be able to save Charles, Debbie, and Thomas.

Jumping to his feet, he told Pedro to help him. Pulling two boards from a corner of the room, he slid each one under the corners of the stove and told Pedro to lift. Together, they moved it aside, exposing a rough-cut trapdoor. It was an escape pit he had been working on, but had never finished. For now, it was nothing more than a hole in the ground, but it was located at the back edge of the house. A person would only have to dig out a short distance, then up, to be free of the house. Jerking the trapdoor open, Zack called Debbie and Thomas to him. Hugging each child tightly, he kissed each on the forehead, then lowered them into the makeshift hiding place. He then called Charles to his side.

"Son, I want you to get down there with the young'uns. We're going to put this stove back in place. You take this bowie knife with you. Once this is over and these men have done left, you use the knife to dig your way out of there. It ain't far. I know you can do it."

Charlie started to protest. "But Pa, I wanta . . ."

Zack cut him off quickly. "Charlie, we ain't got time to argue. You get down there with your brother and sister. An' no matter what you hear going on up here, you all stay real quiet until it's all over an' you hear these men ride away. You hear me, son?"

"Yes, sir."

Martha gave her son a hug and kissed his cheek. Tears were streaming down her face as he lowered himself under the floor and her husband closed the door. Then Zack, Pedro, and Martha gathered all the children's clothes and toys and shoved them into the stove. If there were no signs of children having lived in the house, the Covington children might just stand a chance.

Zack reached out and pulled his wife to him. They held each other tightly for a long time. Pedro, his own eyes filling with water, turned away, feeling awkward and out of place at this solemn moment. He had been with the Covington family for twenty years. They had always treated him well, as if he were a member of their family. He said a silent prayer for them all. Breaking the embrace, the couple stood. Zack took his rifle from its place against the wall. Martha and Pedro did the same.

Smiling at them, Zack said, "I don't suppose any of us want to surrender to these sonsabitches, right?"

Martha frowned. "Zachary Covington. You know how I feel about cursing in my home!"

Shaking his head, he almost laughed, but knew better.

"Sorry, Mother. Guess I got a little carried away. What'd you say we go out there an' give these boys a lesson in Texas manners?"

"Sí, compadre," said Pedro. "Like we used to do in the old days."

Martha levered a round into her Henry rifle. "It's been a good life, Zack. Thank you."

Pedro threw the door open and the trio walked out onto the porch. The Comancheros began to come out of their hiding places, riders approaching from the barn. They had mistakenly taken the exit from the house as a sign of surrender. As a group of them approached, Zack yelled out.

"Now!"

The surprised bandits began to drop like flies as a storm of lead came at them. But it was only a temporary victory. The Comancheros quickly recovered and within a matter of seconds, returned a devastating barrage of their own. Mainly directed at the men. Zack was the first to go down, then Pedro, both men hit more than eight times. As they lay dead at Martha's feet, the veteran frontier woman continued to fire. A bullet tore through her right arm; another drove itself through her left leg. Still another pierced her side. She fell to the ground, her rifle empty.

The rider with the paint looked around the yard. Seven more of his men lay dead. There was anger in his face as he walked the horse up to Martha, who lay bleeding on the ground. One of his men placed the barrel of a rifle against her head and was about to fire.

"No!" he shouted. "That would be too quick." As he stared down at her from his horse, the man's face suddenly transformed into a wicked smile.

"You have killed seven more of my men, you devil-bitch. By the time we are through with you, it is you who will wish for death. Take her inside and strip her naked. I shall be first, then all of you will have a turn—two or three if you like. Go!"

Two men grabbed Martha by the front of her dress and pulled her up the steps and into the house. Seconds later, there was the sound of laughter and clothes being torn away. But Martha never screamed—her children were hiding under the floor.

Pablo Chacon raped Martha first. He was brutal in his attack, wanting to hear this gringo woman scream and cry for mercy, but no matter what he did to her, she never made a sound, even when he pushed a finger into the bullet hole in her side. It spoiled his fun. Having finished with her, he turned her over to the others and walked out onto the porch. One of the Comancheros, a half-breed Comanche called Dog, came up to Chacon and asked what he wanted done with the bodies of Zack and Pedro. Chacon told him to strip them and hang them by their heels from the archway sign at the entrance to the ranch. Dog smiled his approval.

"Can I take my souvenirs?"

Chacon laughed. "Why not? They won't have need of them anymore."

A couple of the men came out of the house, having had their turn with Martha. They each rolled a cigarette and lit up. They were both American cowboys and both wanted by the law. The tall one, a gunman named Mitch Lee, stood just over six feet and had coal-black hair and snapping brown eyes. The other man was stocky, about five-nine, with dirty-blond hair and blue eyes. He was Frank Taggart, a gunman out of Arizona.

"How'd we make out, Chacon?" asked Lee.

Chacon put a match to a cigar as he replied, "Not bad. About forty good horses and close to four hundred head of prime beef. But it'll get better as we move up the Rio Grande. Bigger ranches up that way."

"Yeah, but once the word's out about what happened here, that'll mean Texas Rangers too," said Taggart.

Chacon laughed. "You worry too much, my friend. These Texas Rangers you talk about can die like any other men. I do not fear them—neither should you. We will deal with them the same as we do the Mexican soldiers. A few well-prepared ambushes and dead men should soon discourage them."

Taggart looked over at Lee and shook his head. Chacon was young, and a hothead to boot. He obviously hadn't had very many run-ins with Texas Rangers. If he had, he wouldn't be talking like that. But then, this was the twenty-three-year-old man's first opportunity to lead a raid into Texas. Big Bill Purvis, the boss of the Comanchero raiders, had figured it was time the young son of his dead partner, Hector Chacon, started carrying his part of the load and learning the finer points of being a leader. As an added precaution, Big Tom had sent Lee and Taggart along to help him out and to offer up any advice if he should run into a problem. But that had not been necessary. The younger Chacon demonstrated the ruthless cutthroat qualities of his dead father. His treatment of the woman inside had been a good example of that.

Staring out toward the main gate to the ranch, Taggart saw the naked bodies of Zack Covington and Pedro Cruz slowly rise up from the ground as the ropes around their feet were pulled tight, then tied off at the gate.

Suddenly, there was a bloodcurdling scream from inside the house, then a gunshot. Chacon and the other two men ran into the house. Seven of the raiders were standing around the bed laughing and pointing at the floor as they watched another of the men screaming and flopping about like a chicken with its head cut off. His pants were down and his hands were clutching his privates. Blood was oozing between the fingers. Martha Covington lay naked on the bed, a bullet hole in her chest. She was dead.

"What the hell happened?" shouted Chacon.

One of the men stopped laughing long enough to explain.

"Gawddamn breed there figured he didn't wanta be takin' no poke after nine or ten other fellas, so he stepped up there and stuck his little bitty thing in her mouth and she bit down on it. Had to shoot her to get him loose. But it was too late. She done bite it clean off 'fore she died."

Chacon began to laugh along with the others. "Guess we'll have to be calling him Little Dick from now on."

This brought another roar of laughter from the raiders. A few minutes later, Chacon told them to get the man outside and do what they could for him. When they got ready to leave, someone was going to have to tie him in the saddle. Taggart stared down at the woman on the bed. Her hair was a mess and there was blood on her face, but even in death he noted a certain look of defiance in her lifeless eyes. In her own way, she had fought them to her last breath. As a sign of respect, Taggart picked up a blanket from the floor and covered her.

Chacon told his men they had five minutes to grab whatever they wanted from the ranch. It was time to go. As one of the men came out of the house carrying some bright-colored cloth, Chacon noticed the man was also carrying a rag doll. Chacon stopped him.

"Where did you get that?"

"Found it stuck behind the wood box."

Another man came onto the porch, a flaming torch in his hand. He was preparing to set the house ablaze. Chacon stopped him and taking the torch, told the man to mount up, that he would take care of the house.

Chacon signaled for Taggart and Lee to join him. The three men walked off the porch and whispered among themselves for a moment. Then Chacon shouted, "Amigos, it is time. Let's ride."

As Chacon mounted the paint, he watched the flames roar to life as fire swept over the barn. Coal-black smoke rose toward the sky as the bunkhouse was the next thing to go. Beyond the gate, his men were already heading the horses back toward the Rio Grande. Dust rising from beyond the ridge to the north signaled that the cattle were on the move as well. *"Vámonos, amigos!"*

As the Comancheros rode out of the gate, a few of them

drew their pistols and fired into the bodies hanging from the archway. Their laughter could be heard in the distance as the raiders disappeared into the foothills.

Beneath the floor, Charlie had struggled to remain calm. He had heard the foul talk and the horrible sounds coming from above. The grunting and groaning, the squeaking of the bedsprings, mixed with the laughter of disgusting men cheering on their friends as they ravished his mother. If it had not been for Debbie and Thomas, he would have dug his way clear and tried to kill as many of them as he could before he died. But he did have a sister and a brother. They were all that remained of the Covington family now. As the oldest, he had a duty to protect them and see to it that they somehow survived this ordeal.

Debbie wiped the tears from her eyes and whispered, "Charlie. Are they gone?"

Charlie placed his finger to his lips. "Quiet, Deb. I think I heard them riding away. But we'll wait for a while to be sure."

The passing minutes seemed like hours to the children. Finally, Charlie took the bowie knife and began to work it into the dirt next to him. Slowly digging and scooping the loose dirt aside, cutting a hole large enough for him to squeeze into, he began working his way out from under the house. When he was sure he had gone far enough, he began to stab the blade upward. Dirt fell into his face and mouth. Ignoring it, he continued to dig, knowing that only a few feet away the sweet smell of fresh air and clear blue sky awaited them.

The knife blade suddenly broke the surface. Fresh air filled the hole, giving them all a sense of new life. Charlie began to slash and stab at the opening now, widening the hole ever larger, until at last he was bathed in sunlight and he could see clearly the faces of his sister and little brother. Clawing at the dirt, he finally had the hole wide enough for him to raise his head up out of the ground. Carefully, he eased himself up and looked around at what he could see of the ranch. It was quiet. Not a sound could be heard. He didn't see anyone, but then he was in the back of the house. But he felt sure that the raiders had left. He felt Thomas tugging on his pants leg and crying to be let out of the hole. Telling the boy to back up so the dirt wouldn't get in his eyes, Charlie cut away at the dirt until he could finally work his shoulders out of the hole. Once clear, he crawled out, then reaching back, pulled his brother and sister up into the sunlight. Reaching down into the hole, he grabbed the end of his rifle and brought it up out of the hole.

As soon as the weapon was clear of the hole, it was suddenly jerked from his hands.

"Don't reckon you'll be needin' that, boy!"

Charlie turned to see Mitch Lee and Frank Taggart staring down at him. Lee had Debbie and Thomas by the arm, holding on to them tight.

"Get on up, boy," said Taggart, who drew his gun and fired two shots in the air.

Charlie felt his heart sink as he saw Chacon and his raiders come riding back over the hill. It had been a trick and he had fallen for it. That was why they hadn't burned the house. They had somehow figured out that there were children hiding somewhere on the ranch. And Charlie had heard enough talk about Comancheros to know that children captives were as good as having gold.

As Chacon approached, Charlie asked Taggart, "Could I see my mother before you take us away?"

Taggart shook his head. "You don't want to see your mom, son. Not now."

Chacon's face flashed a wide smile as he took in the full figure of Debbie Covington. She was only fourteen, but had began to develop early on. Her figure, along with her long corn silk–blond hair and those deep blue eyes, made her a prize worth more than all the cattle on the Covington ranch. And the two boys both looked strong and fit. They would bring a good price as well.

"Bring the girl here. She will ride with me. Put the boys up behind the other men," said Chacon.

As Lee released Thomas in order to swing Debbie up to Chacon, Charlie grabbed the man's Colt .45 from its holster. Bringing the hammer back, he pointed the gun straight at Chacon's head. Guns were drawn and hammers went back. So many in fact that it sounded like a convention of crickets.

"Now, you put my sister down, you sonofabitch, or I'll blow your head clean off. The rest of you, get your hands high," said Charlie.

Chacon noted that the barrel of the gun the boy was holding never wavered. There was no doubt in his mind this boy would pull the trigger. Slowly, Chacon lowered Debbie back down to the ground.

"Now what do we do?" asked Chacon. "We are thirty, you are one. I admire your courage, boy, but you are playing a dangerous game here. Now give the gun back and we can be on our way."

Swinging the gun barrel in the direction of the two men sitting next to Chacon, Charlie told them to get off their horses. They looked to their leader. Chacon nodded for them to do as the boy said. Taking the reins, Charlie backed away from the group and told Debbie and Thomas to mount up. From the back of the pack of raiders, Dog eased his horse forward a little at a time, slowly working his way to the front. His hands were still held as high as the others.

Once Debbie and Thomas were set, Charlie told them to head out. He would hold the men there for as long as he could.

"But Charlie, you have to come with us," cried Debbie. "Please, Charlie."

Dog had waited patiently for just the right moment. That moment came as Charlie looked away from the group for an instant and into his sister's eyes. It was only for a second, but it was long enough. Dog's fingers gripped the tip of the blade that rested at the back of his neck, and with the mere flip of the wrist, the breed sent the eight-inch knife through the air and deep into Charlie's heart. The boy took a deep breath. His last. There was a surprised look on his face as the gun dropped from his hand and he fell face-first into the Texas dirt. Dog let out a wild Comanche scream as the others cheered his ability with a blade.

Debbie screamed. Leaping from her horse, she hurried to her brother's side. Taggart grabbed her arm and pulled her away.

"Nothin' you can do for him now, little girl."

Hooking his big hands under her arms, Taggart swung her up in front of Chacon.

"Think we better be movin'," said the gunman. "That smoke can be seen for miles."

Chacon nodded, then told Dog to fire the house and hang the boy at the gate with the others. The Comanche dropped from his horse. Moving to Charlie, he rolled the boy over with the toe of his foot and withdrew his knife.

Wiping the bloody blade on his pants, he told the others to go. He would finish what had to be done.

As the Comancheros rode away, Dog tossed a torch into the house and watched as the flames began to consume it. Placing Charlie's body over his horse, he walked the animal to the gate. Stripping the boy of his clothes, he fastened a rope around Charlie's feet and tied the other end to his horse. Leading the horse forward, until the boy hung next to his father, Dog tied the rope off on a gatepost.

Swinging up onto his horse, Dog stopped beside Charlie's body. Pulling his knife, he cut the boy's ears off and shoved his souvenirs into a leather pouch as he rode away.

TWO

✷

A FULL MOON was rising as John Thomas Law walked his big buckskin, Toby, down the bank and into the middle of the dry riverbed. He followed the winding, twisting bed for a mile, the sand concealing any sound of his approach. When he came to a fork in the riverbed, he brought Toby to a halt, swung his big six-foot-two frame out of the saddle, and stepped down. Tying the reins off to a small blackjack tree, Law reached up and pulled his Winchester .44-40 rifle from the saddle boot. Moving to the gentle slope that ran along the right side of the riverbed, he slowly made his way up to the rim.

The full moon was high now, its radiant glow providing enough light for him to see the run-down cabin located thirty yards to his front. There was a faint light coming through one of the windows. To the right, in a makeshift corral, were three horses. One was an Appaloosa. All three horses had been stolen from a farm north of Denison, Texas. The owner and his wife had been left dead on the front porch of their small place. J.T. had buried the couple, spoken a few words over them, then set out after the trio of killers and bank robbers he had been chasing for three weeks.

Texas Jack Collins was the leader of the bunch. A burly, foul-mouthed, hard case who thought nothing of shooting women or children. He was as bad a stone-cold killer as had ever come out of Texas. He had proved that a month ago when he and his two partners, Ben Johnson and Dutch Henry Brown, held up a bank in Killeen, Texas. They had ridden away with close to thirty thousand dollars, leaving two bank employees dead in the bank and four more innocent people dead in the street. Two of them women.

The outlaws had hightailed it north for the Red River. Word of the killings and the robbery were wired to law-enforcement officers to the north, along with descriptions of the wanted men. Nothing was heard of them for two weeks. Then, outside of Denton, Texas Jack and his boys had stumbled onto a posse looking for rustlers. The lawmen in the group had recognized them from the descriptions in the earlier telegram. In no time, lead was flying and the trio was on the run. In the melee that followed, Jack had his horse shot out from under him, but Brown and Johnson had managed to hold off the posse until their leader could climb up behind Dutch Henry and they made a break for it. The posse lost their trail after dark, and soon gave up and returned home. J.T. had just ridden into town as the posse was coming in. When he asked, the sheriff told him the story of the encounter, and provided information about the general vicinity where they had lost the trail.

The lawman wished J.T. luck in his pursuit, but offered no assistance. That was fine with the gunfighter and bounty hunter. He preferred working alone. Three days of tracking had led him to the tragic discovery at the farm. Two worn-out and broken-down horses had been left in the barn. Horses that had belonged to Johnson and Brown. J.T. followed the trail north from the farm until he came to the small town of Elmont. There, he told the sheriff about the murders at the farm. John Law learned that the couple's name had been Taylor and that Robert Taylor's favorite horse had been a big Appaloosa.

From the trail he'd been following, J.T. figured that Texas Jack was headed for the Red River and the relative safety of Indian Territory, a place that proved to be a haven for every type of outlaw and badman west of the Mississippi. J.T. Law seldom left the state of Texas in his pursuit of a wanted man, but he was willing to make an exception in Texas Jack Collins's case. Someone had to put an end to the man's senseless killing.

He saw the small light in the window go out. The outlaws had finally settled in for the night. He was tempted to go against the odds and his experience and try to take the men now in the dark confines of the small cabin, but one mistake and that could prove fatal. As much as he wanted to be finished with this business, logic told him he would have to wait for daylight and take on the three men once they all came out and gathered at the corral to saddle their horses.

Resting the barrel of the Winchester in the fork of a blackjack tree, J.T. rolled over onto his back and stared up at the big yellow moon and the star-studded sky. He

"Now you put my sister down, you sonofabitch, or I'll blow your head clean off. . . ."

". . .The rest of you, get your hands high," said Charlie.

Chacon noted that the barrel of the gun the boy was holding never wavered. There was no doubt in his mind this boy would pull the trigger. Slowly, Chacon lowered Debbie back down to the ground.

"Now what do we do?" asked Chacon. "We are thirty, you are one. I admire your courage, boy, but you are playing a dangerous game here. Now give the gun back and we can be on our way."

Swinging the gun barrel in the direction of the two men sitting next to Chacon, Charlie told them to get off their horses. They looked to their leader. Chacon nodded for them to do as the boy said. Taking the reigns, Charlie backed away from the group and told Debbie and Thomas to mount up. Once they were set, Charlie told them to head out. He would hold the men there for as long as he could . . .

DON'T MISS THESE
ALL-ACTION WESTERN SERIES
FROM THE BERKLEY PUBLISHING GROUP

THE GUNSMITH by J. R. Roberts
> Clint Adams was a legend among lawmen, outlaws, and ladies. They called him . . . the Gunsmith.

LONGARM by Tabor Evans
> The popular long-running series about Deputy U.S. Marshal Long—his life, his loves, his fight for justice.

SLOCUM by Jake Logan
> Today's longest-running action Western. John Slocum rides a deadly trail of hot blood and cold steel.

BUSHWHACKERS by B. J. Lanagan
> An action-packed series by the creators of *Longarm*! The rousing adventures of the most brutal gang of cutthroats ever assembled—Quantrill's Raiders.

DIAMONDBACK by Guy Brewer
> Dex Yancey is Diamondback, a Southern gentleman turned con man when his brother cheats him out of the family fortune. Ladies love him. Gamblers hate him. But nobody pulls one over on Dex . . .

WILDGUN by Jack Hanson
> The blazing adventures of mountain man Will Barlow— from the creators of *Longarm*.

TEXAS TRACKER by Tom Calhoun
> Meet J. T. Law: the most relentless—and dangerous—man-hunter in all Texas. Where sheriffs and posses fail, he's the best man to bring in the most vicious outlaws—for a price.

and Ol' Man Moon were longtime friends, and J.T. had conversed with him many times in many places over the years. It had become a kind of ritual. A way to pass the time and reflect on memories long past. Like the night a young man in his early twenties named John Thomas Law had vowed his love for a young woman named Sara Jane Woodall. Ol' Man Moon had been as full and bright then as he was on this night. That had been a joyous time, but one that would not last. For as strong as they felt their love to be, it had failed to withstand the turmoil of a nation divided by the War Between the States.

It was this same moon that had cast its glow down on a twenty-three-year-old Quantrill raider, bloodied by war and on the verge of death in a Kansas cornfield. That night, he had stared up at the huge yellow ball in the night sky in pain and wonder and amazement, figuring that it would be the last time he would ever see the moon in all its glory. But he had survived the cornfield and the war itself, only to return home to Texas and find his parents had passed on. The family home was a shambles, the land taken over by carpetbaggers, loathsome snakes who served as agents for wealthy Northern bankers. It was a dark time for Texas. Corrupt politicians were placed in powerful positions by a vengeful Yankee Government and backed by the force of Federal troops. They stole all they could, while at the same time assuring that the residents of the rebellious Southern state were kept in poverty and misery.

Penniless, resentful, and bitter, J.T. had left his beloved Texas, and was soon reunited with a group of his former guerrilla raiders from Missouri. The war might have been over for the regular soldiers of the North and South, but for the men that had ridden with William Quantrill and

Bloody Bill Anderson, it had simply gone into another phase. Their status had changed from Southern raiders to renegade outlaws and killers. They hunted, hounded and pursued by an unforgiving government. Those who had attempted to put aside their guns and return to a normal life had soon discovered that for them, the war would never be over.

Joining his former comrades-in-arms, John Law had sought retribution against the rich Northern bank owners he felt had stolen his home and been the chief architects of the destruction of Texas. Riding alongside his old friends, Jesses and Frank James and the Younger brothers, he soon found himself robbing banks. If the Federal Government wanted to continue its war against the raiders, then so be it. At least this time he'd be well paid for it.

A wanted man by the age of twenty-six, J.T. Law had amassed a small fortune from his time with the James boys. Feeling he had what he was after, he bade his friends farewell and returned to Texas with the hope of buying back his home and reuniting with his Sara. He found things had changed while he had been away. The carpetbaggers and Federal troops were finally gone. There were still signs of poverty, but new hope had been found in the form of longhorn cattle. The North was crying out for beef, and Texas had countless thousands of the wild, longhorn beast. Cattle drives north were beginning to pump new life into Texas. He had hoped to buy back the family ranch with the money stolen from the same bankers who had taken the property to start with, but that was not to be. The Law Ranch had been sold off in sections, and was no longer a ranch at all, but now the property of immigrant farmers who had swarmed into Texas after the war.

As hard as it was to lose the ranch, it was nothing compared to the devastation he felt when he finally went to see Sara. Too many years had passed between them. His letters to her at the beginning of the war had slowly diminished, until finally they had stopped all together. For four long years, she had heard nothing from him. Time and separation had taken its toll. She no longer cared for him, and told him so.

Disillusioned with the path his life had taken, J.T. began to drink, womanize, and gamble until his life spiraled out of control. Ol' Man Moon had borne witness to the destruction of a once-proud man. His money gone, he ended up a penniless drunk, sweeping out saloons for food and sleeping in alleyways. John Thomas Law had become a pitiful sight indeed.

Then, one night, having hustled drinks at different saloons all over town, a drunken, stumbling J.T. Law had wandered out behind a saloon to throw up, when he suddenly slipped and tumbled into a small creek that ran behind the saloon. Lying in the water, so drunk he couldn't even pull himself out of the creek, which was only a foot deep, he simply lay there with the cold water rippling over him and looked up at his old friend the moon. He stared at it for a long time. The longer he stared, the stronger the memories became, so strong, in fact, that they began to overcome the alcoholic stupor he was in. He saw Sara's face, heard Bloody Bill Anderson cussing Yankee troops as he cut them down in battle, saw his friends Cole Younger and Frank James laughing at Jesse that time he fell off his horse. Maybe it was the moon or the icy cold waters of the creek that made these images so clear at that moment, he wasn't sure, but whatever it was, that moment in time changed his life forever.

The man who crawled from that creek on his hands and knees that night was no longer the weak, crumbling shell of a man filled with uncertainty and self-pity. It was as if he had been reborn and with that rebirth, had been restored to his sense of pride and determination. His name was John Thomas Law and he was a Texan—and a Texan didn't know the meaning of the words "give up." He stopped drinking the whiskey, got himself cleaned up, and soon took a job as a mule skinner, hauling freight for a big outfit out of Dallas. It didn't really pay all that well, but it was good honest work and he stayed with it for almost a year.

One day, he was playing cards with some of the other teamsters. Looking out the window, they saw a man leading a horse toward the sheriff's office. There was a body draped over the saddle. One of the men at the table recognized the man leading the horse, and identified him as a gunman who hunted down wanted men for the rewards. He was a professional bounty hunter. Talk around the table was that it was a risky business, but if a man was good with a gun and trail-smart, he could make a lot of money. There was no shortage of outlaws and hard cases roaming Texas with a price on their head. All a man needed was the grit to go out and get them.

That day, John Thomas Law quit his job as a teamster and began a journey into a whole new life as a bounty man. At last, this was something he knew he could do. After having ridden with Bloody Bill in the war and later with his guerrilla comrades, Frank James and Cole Younger, he had no doubt he had the grit and the sand to go after a man on a wanted poster.

An so began the career of John Thomas Law as bounty hunter. He soon found that it was a life that suited him well. His abilities with a gun had been honed during the war. But it wasn't until he got his hands on a Colt .45 Peacemaker that J.T. Law reached his full potential as a gunfighter. Constant practice with the new gun soon earned him a reputation as one of the deadliest men in Texas. Over the years, that reputation had grown to include his talent as a bounty hunter.

For an outlaw, his worst nightmare would be to find John Thomas Law was on his backtrail. Ever vigilant and determined, once he started after a man, he didn't stop until he caught up to him. The wanted man was always given a choice: surrender and go along peaceably, or try his luck with the iron on his hip. It was this option that set J.T. Law apart from other bounty men. He had never shot a man in the back or from ambush. Every man that he had put in the ground had been given a chance at a fair fight. It was this difference that had earned him the respect of a number of Rangers and lawmen, and even a few outlaws themselves.

Sam Bass, leader of one of the most successful outlaw gangs in Texas, had been quoted by a Dallas newspaper once as saying that if he ever got cornered by the law or bounty hunters, he hoped John T. Law was among them. At least then he knew he'd be given "a fair shake and a chance for a fair fight."

J.T. had come a long way over the years, and was still alive when so many others had died. Wild Bill had been shot in the back of the head in Deadwood. George Custer had finally let all that glory nonsense outweigh logic and gotten himself, and a large part of the Custer clan, killed, along with some fine damn cavalrymen, at the Bighorn River up in Dakota territory. Cole, Jim, and Bob Younger were in prison up Minnesota for their part in the failed bank robbery in Northfield. Cell Miller, Charlie Pitts, and Bill Chadwell had been killed in the same robbery attempt. Jesse and Frank had been the only two members of the gang to escape, and nothing more had been heard about them since that fateful day.

He often wondered how he had managed to survive so long since he had become a bounty man, but he had, and along the way he had taken the lives of twenty men. Once morning came, either he would be dead, or three men would be added to that number. True to his reputation, J.T. would give all three the chance to surrender, but he had learned over the years that few men who took up the outlaw way of life were willing to give up their freedom for a four-by-eight cell or the terrible ordeal of a long drop with a short rope around their neck.

Texas Jack, Ben Johnson, and Dutch Henry Brown were all hard men who had freely chosen the dangerous and often desperate life of outlaws. As mean and deadly as they were, J.T. understood them. And why not? At one time, he himself had been one of them. He had discovered early on that there was nothing romantic or exciting about being chased all over the country by posses and Pinkertons, or running a cold camp where fixing a fire to make coffee to ward off a freezing night might well bring down the wrath of a posse that spotted the fire or the smoke. Nothing romantic about sleepless nights on the cold ground spent worrying that every sound in the dark might be a signal that the law was sneaking up on you or waiting to ambush you at first light. What kind of men would want to live a life like that? He had only done it for two years, but that had been enough for him.

He knew if he hadn't left Jesse and Frank when he did, he would have been lying in the street of Northfield, Min-

nesota, along with Charlie Pitts and the others. No, as
much as he would like to think he could take these three
men back to Texas without a fight, the reality was this
was going to be a fight to the death. They would not
surrender. These were men who expected to face death
every day. They wouldn't really be surprised to see him
in the morning. If it wasn't him, it would be a posse or a
lawman somewhere else. As the moon passed across the
night sky, J.T. bade his old friend good night and drifted
off to sleep.

The blowing sand against his face woke J.T. just before
dawn. As he rubbed at his eyes, he rolled over and inched
his way up to the rim. The wind was picking up, and he
could barely see the outline of the cabin in the distance.
In the corral, the horses were moving around nervously,
seeking someplace to go to get out of the blowing wind
and the stinging sand. They began to whinny and rear up,
kicking at the makeshift corral. A light suddenly appeared
in the cabin. Then the door opened. A tall figure came
out and made his way to the horses. Soon after, a second
figure appeared and covering his head with his coat, ran
to the corral to help. They were going to take the horses
inside the cabin. Otherwise, the animals might bust up the
makeshift corral and run off.

As the dawn quickly began to lengthen across the
morning sky, J.T. grabbed up his rifle and using the
blowing sand as cover, moved far to the left and began
working his way toward the back of the cabin. As he
made it to the back wall of the place, he rubbed furiously
at his eyes to try to get the sand out of them. The wind
had picked up even more by now. The biting grains of
sand stung his face and hands. Pulling his cowskin vest
off, J.T. placed it over his head and knelt next to the cabin,

huddling as close to the wall as he could get and placing his hands inside his shirt. He could hear voices yelling inside and the stomping of the nervous horses.

Each passing minute seemed like an eternity to the bounty man as the sandstorm grew in intensity. It lasted for nearly an hour. Then, as quickly as it had appeared, it was gone. The sun was up and there wasn't a cloud in the sky. Slowly pulling the vest from his head, J.T. stood up. Only moments ago, the roaring wind and biting sand had made it impossible for him to hear anything. Now it was dead still. There wasn't even a breeze blowing. Shaking the sand from his hat and clothes, J.T. cleared the sand from around the chamber of the Winchester and began moving along the left wall toward the front of the cabin. There were no back or side doors. The only way out was the front. Reaching the corner of the building, he took off his hat and peered around the end of the logs, toward the door. Pulling his head back, he rested his back against the wall and waited.

It wasn't a long wait. He heard the door creak as it was opened. Then one of the men said, "It's cleared off. Let's get 'em saddled."

J.T. pressed back against the wall, and didn't move as the three men walked right past him, leading their horses to the saddles and rigging hanging on the corral. He recognized Texas Jack by the black low-crowned, wide-brimmed hat and black vest he was known for wearing. The first man at the corral grabbing up his saddle was Ben Johnson. As he turned to swing the outfit up onto his horse, he saw John T. standing at the corner of the cabin, his Winchester leveled at the trio.

"Goddamn! We're caught, boys!" he shouted.

Texas Jack and Dutch Henry released their horses and

whirled around to see what Johnson was talking about.
J.T. stepped forward away from the cabin. Dutch made a
motion as if he were going to try for his gun. J.T. raised
the rifle. "You're welcome to give a try, friend. But I
wouldn't if I was you."

Texas Jack slowly raised his hands as he said, "Ya got
no chance against that Winchester, Dutch. Best let it go.
I reckon he's got us fair and square."

"Okay, boys. Let's lose that hardware. Left hand—drop
the gunbelts," said J.T.

Jack and Dutch reached low and undid the tie-downs
around their legs, then slowly reached across with their
left hands and began to unhitch their gunbelts. At the
same time, Ben Johnson, still holding his saddle, bent over
to place it on the ground. As he started to raise up, he
suddenly had a gun in his hand. The reward notice had
failed to mention that Johnson always carried a hideaway
in a special holster on the side of his saddle.

The sight of the gun took John T. totally by surprise.
Before he knew it, Johnson sent a round into the wall
next to his head. At the same instant, Law triggered the
Winchester, sending a .44-40 slug through the man's
chest. The impact sent Johnson backward into the corral,
which collapsed around the dead man's body.

Jack and Dutch had both drawn their guns and were
firing now. J.T. felt a sudden burn along his right shoulder
as a bullet tore through his shirt. Another round hit his
Winchester and sent it careening out of his hands. Drawing his Peacemaker with lightning speed, he dived forward in the sand, firing two shots before he hit the ground.
Dutch Henry staggered, then tried to lift his gun for another shot, but the two bullets in his chest put an end to
that effort and to his life. As he watched Dutch Henry

crumple to the sand, Texas Jack screamed, "Ya sonofabitch!" then began firing wildly at J.T. as the gunfighter
rolled along the ground. If he'd taken his time, Jack might
have had a chance of hitting his target, but his rage, and
possibly his fear, sent the bullets harmlessly into the sand
until finally, when he pulled the trigger and heard the
hammer of his .45 click as it fell on a spent cartridge,
Texas Jack Collins was out of bullets.

J.T. stood up and dusted himself off as the outlaw
yelled, "Well, go on, damnit! Get it over with. Finish me
off. What the hell ya waitin' for?"

John T. holstered his gun. "No, Jack. I'm not going to
kill you. I'm taking you back. Some folks back there got
a rope waitin' for you."

The very thought of hanging brought fear to the hard
case's face. Collins was a big man, a little over six feet
and close to 230 pounds. Lowering his head, he charged
John T., hoping to take him down, but J.T. was ready for
that. As the raging bull of a man reached out for him, the
gunfighter sidestepped and drove a fist into Jack's gut.
J.T. heard the air go out of the man. With the man still
bent over, J.T. stepped in and brought his knee up into
Jack's face with all his might. The bone-shattering blow
sent the big man backward and off his feet. He hit the
sand with a thud. He didn't move. He was out cold. A
stream of bright red blood soaked the front of his shirt as
it flowed from his broken nose.

By the time Jack came to, he found himself mounted
and tied to his saddle. The rope extended behind to the
other two horses, which were carrying the bodies of Ben
Johnson and Dutch Henry Brown. His horse was being
led by J.T. Law, who was now riding a big buckskin.
Jack's nose hurt like hell, and every step the horse took

caused him pain, but even with that, he yelled out, "Hey, just who the hell are ya anyway, mister?"

J.T. looked back over his shoulder. "John Thomas Law."

Texas Jack Collins managed a laugh as he said, "Damn! Well, I reckon if I gotta be caught by somebody, I'd want it to be the best. Ain't no shame in bein' caught by the likes of ya, John T. Law. Folks'll remember that too when I'm on them gallows. Yes, sir. They'll be sayin' it took John T. Law himself to corral ol' Texas Jack Collins, an' that'll be fine. Yes, sir. Mighty fine."

THREE

★

JOHN LAW'S ENTRANCE into the town of Denison, Texas, caused major excitement among the townspeople. The sight of Texas Jack hogtied and the two bodies draped over the saddles was something none of them had ever expected to see. When they discovered who it was who had captured the outlaws, they were even more excited. The famous gunfighter and bounty hunter John T. Law was in their town. Practically everyone had heard of the man, but none had ever seen him in person. Any doubts about the stories of this man's courage and ability with a gun were quickly set aside. The proof was right before their eyes. One man had gone up against three of the toughest men in Texas at the same time and bested all three.

The young women of the town seemed particularly interested in the man. He stood six feet three, with broad shoulders and a narrow waist. His hair was black and the eyes were blue-green. The face was handsome in a manly way. He had a strong-looking jaw and perfect nose that fit him well. The slightest trace of a dimple when he smiled seemed to drive the ladies to the verge of fainting dead away. There was no doubt that John Thomas Law was the most popular man in town on this day.

The sheriff asked Texas Jack if he would verify the identity of his two dead comrades, which he did freely, crediting J.T. with some of the fanciest shooting he had seen since taking up the outlaw trail. The identity confirmed, the sheriff went about filling out the paperwork for the reward money that had been offered by the State of Texas and the bank that had been robbed.

Tired and saddle weary, John Thomas made his way through the crowd of curious onlookers and down the street to the hotel. A young boy about fifteen ran up and offered to stable Toby for him. John T. was too tired to argue, and gave the boy a dollar for his trouble. At the hotel, the owner greeted him at the door. He held a key in his hand and pointed upstairs.

"It's the best room in the place, Mr. Law. With the compliments of the house."

J.T. thanked the man, and started up the stairs as the hotel man told the people to go on about their business and give the weary hero a chance to rest. Reluctantly, the people began to fade away from the front of the hotel.

The room was nice, but all J.T. had on his mind at the time was the big four-poster bed and feather mattress that sat against one wall. Hanging his gunbelt on one of the posts next to the pillow, he sat down, his two hundred pounds sinking into the softness of the mattress. Pulling his boots off, he poured the sand-filled leather into the chamber pot next to a nightstand, then tossed the boots in the corner. Swinging his feet up onto the bed, he fell back into pillows and was sound asleep within minutes.

The knock on the door brought J.T. straight up out of the bed. The Colt Peacemaker was in his hand and the hammer back before his feet hit the floor. Grabbing the gun had been a reflex action, something all gunfighters learned early on in their careers. They could never be sure what fate awaited them on the other side of a closed door. Moving across the room, he quietly slid the bolt open, then stepped to the side of the entranceway.

"Yeah! Who is it?"

The answering voice was a familiar one.

"John Thomas. It's me. Let me in."

J.T. opened the door for his old friend, Abe Covington, captain of a company of Texas Rangers out of Austin.

"Well, I'll be damned. Get in here you ol' horse thief. Long way from home, ain't you?"

The bounty man could see by the look on Abe's face that he wasn't his usual devil-make-care self. Something was wrong. Law watched the six-foot-four bear of a man move across the room. Abe had the broadest shoulders John had ever seen, and the man's arms were as big around as the legs on most men.

"You got a drink?" asked Abe as he dropped down into a chair near the bed. "I'm as dry as a damn creek in July."

J.T. pointed to the nightstand next to the bed.

"Help yourself, Abe. Compliments of the good people of Denison. But watch yourself. It's real whiskey—not that snakebite shit you're used to drinking."

Removing the cap, Abe didn't bother with a glass. Tipping the bottle up, he took a long pull on the whiskey,

then set it aside. John T. crossed the room, slipped the
Colt back into the holster, and sat down on the bed. Taking the bottle from the stand, he poured himself a drink
in a glass and set the bottle back over toward Abe. Just
as J.T. had mastered the gun, he had also mastered his
control over the alcohol. He had never been drunk again
since that night in the cold creek behind the saloon. He
knew his limitations with whiskey and had learned to control his drinking.

"What are you doin' this far north, Abe? You after
somebody?"

Covington's hands suddenly balled into two massive
fists.

"You remember my brother Zack?"

J.T. nodded. Law, Abe, and a small outfit of eight
Rangers had been after a gang of horse thieves last summer. They had trailed them to the Rio Grande, but the
outlaws had already crossed over into Mexico. There was
nothing they could do. On the way back to Austin, the
group had stopped and spent the night at Zack Covington's ranch.

"Sure I remember him, Abe. Got a nice little ranch just
outside Laredo. Wife, Martha, laid out a fine spread for
us when we were there. Best damn biscuits I ever ate. Got
a parcel of kids too, if I remember right."

Abe grabbed up the bottle and took another long drink.
Clutching the bottle in his hand, he leaned forward in the
chair and stared down at the floor.

"They're dead, John T."

John Law's head snapped up and he stared at Abe for
a moment.

"Who's dead, Abe?"

Abe brought his free hand up and rubbed at his eyes.

"Zack, Martha, and their oldest boy, Charlie. Ol' Pedro Cruz, the foreman, and four of the ranch hands. They're all dead. It was a goddamn massacre."

Stunned by the news, J.T. shook his head. "My God, Abe. I'm sorry. When did this happen? Do you know who did it?"

Abe couldn't bring himself to look at the gunfighter. He didn't want J.T. to see the tears that slowly filled his eyes.

"Happened four days ago. Some cowboys from another ranch saw lots of smoke in the sky over toward Zack's place. When they rode over to investigate, they found Zack, Charlie, and Pedro hangin' by their heels from the gate sign. The house and barn were ablaze. Judgin' from the sign they found, the ranch put up a pretty good fight. They found eleven of the sonsabitches scattered out around the barn and the house. Marshal out of Laredo sent the news. They found Martha's body in the house. She'd been on the bed. They didn't say no more about that, but then they didn't have to. Marshal said it looked like maybe thirty or forty riders were in the outfit that attacked the ranch. All the cattle and the horses were gone. They headed for the Rio. A posse went after 'em, but hell, you know how that works. The trail ended at the Rio Grande and so did the marshal's authority."

Abe paused. Taking another drink, he choked back tears as he sighed and said, "They . . . they cut their ears off, John. Why? Why . . . why would a man do a thing like that? You'd think it was enough you killed 'em and hung 'em up like some damn piece of meat. What kind of sick bastard would cut off a man's ears?"

John Law didn't have an answer for his friend.

"Just who the hell were these fellas, Abe? Mexican bandits?"

Abe shook his head, then raised his eyes and looked at J.T.

"Worse. Comancheros."

"Comancheros! Hell, I thought you and the Rangers, along with Colonel Randle Mackenzie's calvary, put an end to that bunch after the Red River War."

"We did. Shut 'em down for good at the Canyon del Rescate. Ol' Juan Trijillo and Jose Tafoya gave it up after that. That was in west Texas. Hadn't been no Comanchero trouble around these parts for years. Somebody has started 'em up again, but they work out of Mexico now. U.S. Army can't bother 'em over there."

J.T. suddenly remembered something. "Abe. Didn't Zack have two other kids? Another boy and a girl, right?"

John Law could tell from the pained expression on the Ranger's face that the question was like a stake through his heart. Abe's voice broke as he spoke.

"Yes. Deb . . . Debbie. She's fourteen now. An' Thomas. He's on . . . only ten. They didn't find them at the ranch. We figure they took the kids with 'em. That's why I'm here, John Thomas. I'm goin' after them kids and I ain't comin' back without 'em. Doubt anybody'd have a snowball's chance in hell of gettin' 'em back, but I gotta try. I owe Zack and Martha that much. Thought maybe if you wasn't busy, you just might wanta come along. Won't be no money in it for you. All I can promise you is plenty of killin' and a damn good chance of dyin'.''

John Thomas Law stood up and strapped on his holster.

"What are we doin' hangin' around here, Abe? Let's ride."

• • •

HIGH IN THE Sierra Madre Mountains of Mexico, Big
Bill Purvis put his arm around Pablo Chacon's neck and
hugged the young man. Through tobacco-stained teeth
and tequila breath, he congratulated Chacon on the suc-
cess of his first raid into Texas. His father Hector would
have been proud to see his son had done so well. The
cattle and horses alone would bring more money than the
total of the last three raids all put together. And the children—there was where the real money was. The boy
would bring a strong price because he was so young and
had a lot of years worth of work in him. The girl, on the
other hand, would bring a considerable fortune. Her long
golden hair and deep blue eyes, along with her budding
young body and flawless skin, made her a prize worthy
of a king's ransom.

The speeches over, the fiesta celebrating Pablo's tri-
umphant return began. The party would last all night, with
plenty of dancing and drinking. Pablo quickly grabbed up
one of the senoritas and with a bottle of tequila, headed
into the crowd of merrymakers, while Big Bill waved for
Mitch Lee and Frank Taggart to follow him up to the main
house. Inside, he pointed the two gunman to his elaborate
and well-stocked liquor cabinet.

Each man grabbed a bottle of aged whiskey and joined
their boss at a huge oak dining-room table that sat near
the double French doors that overlooked the plaza below.

"So tell me. Did you get to see our friend in Laredo?"
asked Purvis.

"Yeah. He said that shipment of new rifles will be coming in next week. He didn't know the exact day yet, but

he'll let us know in plenty of time for us to be ready to steal them from the Army," said Lee.

"You gave him the envelope I sent?"

"Yep. He sent his thanks. But who wouldn't after gettin' ten thousand dollars. Seems kind of high to me, Boss. I mean, the fella don't take any of the risk. He just passes the information along."

"Yeah, Mitch, but it's information we need. An' don't forget, this little setup was his idea. He just didn't have the know-how to put it all together till I come along. You boys stick with me an' I'll make us all rich, by God."

"Hear, hear," said Taggart in a drunken tone as he raised his glass, spilling half his drink on the table. "To Big Bill Purvis—the man with the plan."

They all laughed and tipped their glasses.

"Speaking of plans," said Lee. "What'd you figure to do with that little girl out there? I know she's young, but she's sure bloomin' out all over."

Purvis frowned. "Now, Mitch Lee, you keep away from that girl, you hear me? I don't want her soiled in no way. That little lady's our ace in the hole."

"What the hell you talkin' about, Bill?" asked Lee.

"Who we gonna be sellin' those Army rifles to?" asked Bill.

Taggart threw an arm over the back of his chair as he answered, "Notonte and his Apache renegades. An' for gold too. Right, Bill?"

"That's right, Frank. But I'm gonna raise the price on them rifles this time."

Lee almost spat up his whiskey. "You crazy, Bill? That damn Apache'll cut your throat for you if you try somethin' like that. Notonte ain't nobody to mess with now.

I'm tellin' you for your own good. He thinks you're tryin'
to fuck him over, he'll kill you for sure."

"Not if I throw in that little gal out there as a bonus he
won't." Purvis laughed. "Hell, that big-ass buck's done
wore out two Apache wives and them three Mex gals we
gave him a few months ago. Outside of whiskey and
fighin', Notonte don't like nothin' better than pokin' them
gals. He sees this one, he'll give me any damn thing I
want."

Lee laughed, then said, "Gotta hand it to you, Bill.
You're thinkin' all the time. Ain't that right, Frank?"

Taggart simply nodded in agreement. He'd been getting
pretty drunk, but when Purvis said what he was going to
do with the girl, it had damn near sobered him up and he
wasn't sure why. They'd traded off other kids and women
to Notonte. So why should this one bother him? Maybe
it was just the tequila. Hell with it. Big Bill could do
whatever he wanted. He was the big boss of this outfit.
Frank Taggart wasn't nothing but a hired gun from Arizona, killing time down in old Mexico till something better came along.

Down from the house and across the campgrounds,
stuck away in a dark corner of the compound, was a
wooden cage. Inside, Debbie Covington held her little
brother tight in her arms, and continued to rock him even
though he had gone to sleep twenty minutes ago. She sang
him the same song their mother had sung every night
when she put them to bed. It had been the only thing that
had stopped his crying. Her arms were tired and she could
have laid him down—and she would before long—but
for now, holding him close, with his head against her
chest, was all the comfort the fourteen-year-old girl had
in the world.

Drunken men, and some women, had been coming to the cage all night to peer in at them as if they were animals. They said and did disgusting things as they yelled and laughed at them. Debbie struggled to ignore them, but found it impossible to shut out all the filthy things they said. She could only close her eyes and hold Thomas tightly to her and hope they would all go away. As it got later, fewer and fewer people came to stare at them. Now, as she sat rocking Thomas, it was finally quieting down. The only people moving about were the guards at the house and a few along the canyon walls overlooking the compound.

A tear ran down her face. What was going to happen to them? Her mother, father, and brother Charlie were dead. As fearful as she was now, she knew that this was only the beginning of their ordeal. Her biggest fear was the unknown fate that lay ahead of them. She leaned back against the rough-cut wood. Still holding Thomas tight, the little girl drifted off to sleep.

FOUR

✦

THE HEAT WAS sweltering as Abe and J.T. arrived in Austin. At Ranger headquarters, Abe found a stack of telegrams from every Ranger outfit in Texas. All had heard the news and were volunteering to join up with Abe in whatever action he planned to take against the men that had done this terrible thing to his brother and family. The same was true of the men under his command. Every Ranger of E Company was ready to ride with their captain, to hell if necessary. Chief among them was the youngest Ranger in the company, Billy Tyler, who had arrived in Austin two years earlier as a nineteen-year-old upstart determined to make his mark as a Texas Ranger. In no time, he had proven himself to be one of the best trackers and horsemen in the company. Although short on years, young Billy was long on courage. He had acquitted himself well in gun battles with Indians, bandits, and rustlers. He never forgot that it was Abe Covington who had given him a chance when no one else would. Now his captain needed help and he wanted him to know that he was there for him.

Abe was touched by the outpouring of condolences and offers to join him in this battle, but he also knew that there was no way he could accept the offers. The men he was going after had crossed the border into Mexico. No force, whether it be lawmen or military, could enter Mexico without the permission of the president in Mexico City, and that was not going to happen. There were still plenty of hard feelings between the United States and Mexico. Abe knew that Mexico City would love nothing better than to catch a group of Rangers violating the sanctions of Mexico's border. Not only would the Rangers be subject to Mexican authority, but it would create an international incident that would be an embarrassment to the United States.

If by some miracle they were to be released by the Mexican government, they would then find themselves being arrested by the U.S. government for the violation of the U.S.-Mexico treaty. As much as Covington would welcome the help of his fellow lawmen, he wouldn't be responsible for seeing them lose their lives or face the possibility of prison in Mexico or the United States.

John T. and Abe were going over the map of Mexico when Billy Tyler knocked, then entered the captain's office. Walking straight to Abe's desk, the handsome young man, with blond hair and deep blue eyes, stood his slim, six-foot frame ramrod-straight. Removing the Ranger badge from his shirt, he placed it on the desk.

"Cap'n, sir. Corporal William Tyler hereby resigns

from the Texas Rangers. I do so of my own free will, sir."

J.T. looked over at Abe and couldn't help but smile a little. Abe could only shake his head. They both knew exactly what Billy was up to. Abe lit a cigar and strolled over to his desk. Looking Tyler straight in the eye, he said, "Okay, Mr. Tyler. You wanta tell me what you think you're doing?"

Tyler continued to stare straight ahead. "Sir. I'm resigning. I want to leave the Rangers."

"Horseshit!" said Abe. "An' just what do you plan on doin' once you're out of the Rangers, Mr. Tyler?"

Billy's eyes met the captain's. "Go to Mexico with you and Mr. Law, Cap'n. Ain't no treaty stoppin' American citizens from crossin' into Mexico. Not that I heard tell of anyway. Most of the other boys are married or got family. My folks are dead—I got no brothers or sisters, aunts or uncles—nobody. Just me."

Covington picked up the badge. "Took you a long time to earn this, son. I don't really think you oughta give it up that easy. Now, I appreciate what you're tryin' to do here, Billy, but it ain't worth messin' up your life. So you just put this back on and get outta here."

There was a moment of silence in the room. Billy Tyler wasn't moving. He never flinched or batted an eye as he replied, "Sorry, Cap'n. But I done made up my mind 'bout this. I can rejoin the Rangers when we get back. But I'm comin' along, sir. If not with you, then trailin' a mile or so behind, but I will be there when you need help, sir."

Abe saw John Law smiling again. There wasn't any doubt Tyler would be a welcome addition. He was good with a six-gun, but even more deadly with a Winchester. He had proven that countless times. He was the youngest

Ranger in the outfit, but could outshoot every man-jack of them when it came to the long gun.

Abe looked over at Law. "What the hell do you do with a boy lookin' to get himself killed?"

Tyler and Law exchanged glances. J.T. had worked with the boy before and knew Billy could hold his own in a fight.

"Hell, you invite him along," said Law.

Billy's eyes lit up. His admiration for J.T. Law had just risen ten times higher than normal.

"You sure about this, Billy?" asked Abe.

"Yes, sir, I am. I'd consider it an honor and a privilege to accompany you two fellas anywhere."

Abe slide his desk drawer open and dropped the badge inside. "This'll be here anytime you want it back." Extending his hand across the desk, he shook with Billy. "Just remember, son. You asked to be dealt into this game. I got a feelin' there's goin' be a lot of killin'— hell, there's a damn good chance we'll all get killed ourselves 'fore it's over. It's gonna be a tough fight."

Releasing Abe's hand, the boy simply smiled and answered, "Won't want it any other way."

That settled, the three men studied the map. They had marked the spot on the Rio Grande where the marshal reported the Comancheros had crossed back into Mexico. Beyond lay the Sierra Madres, a vast, rugged mountain range that could hide an entire army. J.T. knew they could cross the border at the same place as the men they were looking for, but after that, they had no idea which way to go. They could search those mountains for a year and never come across the Comanchero camp. This wasn't going to be easy and it was going to take time.

The first thing they were going to have to do was get

some more help. Three men, no matter how good they were with guns, didn't stand a real chance against an army of fifty or sixty veteran fighters like the Comancheros. But by the same token, they couldn't take a large group of twenty or thirty men with them either. That was sure to draw unwanted attention, not only from the people in the area, but from the Mexican military as well. Abe agreed with J.T. on that point. At most, they could get by with perhaps seven. But where were they going to find four men who were willing to ride into Mexico for no pay, face over fifty guns, and risk their lives for a little girl and boy they didn't even know? It seemed highly unlikely such men could be found on such short notice.

J.T. told Abe to get started on the supplies they'd need, while he and Billy went in search of the unlikely. Austin was a big place. It wouldn't hurt to take a look around. It was said Texans were a crazy bunch. There just might be four of them out there somewhere crazy enough to go along.

Together, the two men began visiting the saloons. J.T. heard that the gunfighter and gambler Ben Thompson was in town, but this wasn't Ben's kind of game. J.T. had started out on his mission feeling pretty confident he could find four men for the job, but as they traveled from saloon to saloon, that hope began to dim. Most of the men they found were local folks and cowboys that worked the surrounding ranches. Not the type of men they were going to need for this job.

As they walked up to the bar in one of the few remaining saloons, J.T. ordered a couple of beers, and began wondering if Doc Holliday might still be hanging around Fort Griffin. J.T. and Doc had been involved in a shootout up in Waco a few months ago. Doc had mentioned Fort

Griffin when they had parted company. There was a good chance he would be willing to go along. J.T. knew if he didn't find someone soon, he might just have to send a telegram to Doc.

Billy interrupted J.T.'s thoughts by nudging him with his elbow.

"How about them fellows at the poker table in the corner?" he asked.

John Thomas cast a casual glance in that direction, then suddenly began to smile.

"You look like the cat that caught the bird walkin', J.T. You know them fellas?"

John Law nodded, "Oh, yeah. Them two boys with their backs to the wall are the McMasters brothers, Matt and Harvey. They're both wanted up in Kansas for questioning about a few bank robberies, and here in Texas for the shootin' of a couple of Yankee soldiers. They're both fair hands with a gun."

Billy eyed the two men as he asked, "You going to try and take 'em in?"

"Hell, no. I'm going to go over there and try and convince them to join up with us."

"How you gonna do that, J.T.?"

"Real easy, Billy. They can take a trip to Mexico or spend the next twenty years playin' cards in a Federal prison. Come on, but watch yourself. I don't want no gunplay if we can help it."

Billy shifted his holster slightly just in case, then followed the bounty man across the room toward the table. Matt looked up and saw them approach. He said something, and Harvey looked in their direction as well. J.T. saw Matt's hand start to move below the table.

"Wouldn't do that, Matt. Some of these boys might

think you're cheatin'. What'd you say we just leave the hands above the table. That goes for you too, Harvey," said John Law.

The other three men in the game quickly tossed in their cards, slowly stood, and moved away from the table. Matt looked to be the older, perhaps in his mid-thirties. Harvey was a few years younger. Both men had black hair and dark threatening eyes. Matt brought his hand back up and placed it on his whiskey glass.

"We know you from someplace, mister?"

Billy moved to the left side of Harvey McMasters as J.T. replied, "Saw you boys in a fight down in El Paso once. You took on four drovers in a fistfight at the Grover's Saloon. Handled yourselves damn well too. You two went through them cowboys before they knew what hit 'em."

"Hell," snorted Harvey as he cast a nervous eye toward Billy Tyler. "Is that all this is about—a damn brawl in a saloon?"

J.T. shook his head. "No, I'm afraid not, boys. I hear you fellows took a little trip up Kansas way after El Paso. There's some folks in Ellsworth would like to talk to you about that. Seems one of their banks got robbed about the same time you boys were leaving town. Gave some damn good descriptions too."

Harvey suddenly got more nervous. He shot a worried glance across the table at his brother. Matt didn't say anything, but J.T. saw him shake his head slightly from side to side. A signal to Harvey to keep his mouth shut. J.T. had to give it to him. Matt McMasters was a cool customer. The man took a sip of his whiskey, then set the glass back on the table.

"Yeah, I think we heard somethin' about that a few

days later while we were passin' through Indian Territory. But we don't know nothin' about no bank robbery in Ellsworth, Kansas, friend."

"How about the two dead Yankee troopers from Fort Clark that you boys killed in Brackettville? Guess you left before that happened too, that right?"

Harvey answered before Matt could say anything.

"Now wait a minute. Them soldiers lost their money fair and square in a poker game we was in. When Matt and me went outside, they was layin' for us. They got off two shots 'fore we even pulled iron. Time it was over, they was dead. Town was full of soldiers from the fort. Me and Matt figured them boys would rather hang us than hear the story, so we hightailed it outta there. That's the honest God's truth, mister."

J.T. had seen the flyer on that gunfight and it didn't read anything like that, but during his travels he'd heard the same story Harvey had just told from people that were there that night. Given the situation, J.T. didn't blame them for running. He would have done the same thing.

"You a marshal or somethin'?" asked Matt.

"No—worse. I'm a bounty hunter. Why don't you boys come along with us. I think we need to talk someplace where it's a little more private. Just be careful how you come out of them chairs."

The brothers eyed J.T. and Billy, then exchanged glances. John Law already knew what they had in mind. They weren't going to go for their guns; they were going to handle this with their fists. They had misjudged the toughness of young Billy Tyler. Although twenty-one, he looked more like a kid of seventeen. He was tall and lanky, and there wasn't a lot of meat on that frame, but

J.T. had seen the boy in a scrap. Billy could hold his own with the best of them.

Matt and Harvey bent over and slowly slid their chairs back. As they straightened up, Matt swung on J.T. while Harvey went after Billy. J.T. dodged Matt's big right hand, but was surprised by a roundhouse left that caught him along the left temple and sent him back into another poker table. Matt leaped forward and was on him, delivering a flurry of lefts and rights as fast as he could rain them down on the bounty man. J.T. managed to block most of them, but the ones that got through were solid, teeth-rattling blows. In a surprise move, he grabbed the front of Matt's shirt and pulling the big man forward, delivered a head butt that staggered Matt and made him back off a few steps, giving J.T. a few much-needed seconds to catch his breath and clear his head. He couldn't believe how fast the man was with his hands. He'd known full well what was coming, and he had still been caught off guard by Matt's strength and speed.

At the same time, Billy had sidestepped Harvey's wild swing and hit the big fellow square on the right jaw so hard, the man had gone over the table and hit the floor hard. Billy slung the chairs and table out of his way, and got to Harvey just as the man was halfway up on his feet. Billy let him get upright, then gave him a hard right, followed by an even harder left cross, sending Harvey to the floor once more. The big man shook his head in an effort to clear it. He couldn't figure out where this kid was getting all the power that was behind those blows. Hell, he didn't look like he weighed enough to hit that damn hard. But three loose teeth and a mouthful of blood told Harvey he was wrong about that.

J.T. moved in on Matt with a solid right to the gut that

sent a gush of air out of the man. As he bent over in pain, J.T. brought his knee up, catching Matt full in the face and sending him careening backward into the wall. He wavered there for a moment, his face a bloody mess, then slid down the wall, coming to rest on the floor. He'd had enough.

The same was true of Harvey. Three times he'd gotten up, and three times Billy Tyler had sent him to the floor. For all his cussing and swinging, Harvey hadn't hit the boy once during the whole ruckus. Taking their guns, Billy and J.T. pulled the brothers to their feet and headed them out the door toward Ranger headquarters. Abe was still out rounding up supplies. The brothers saw cells in the back room of Abe's office, and started for them without being told.

"Where you goin', Matt?" asked J.T.

Both brothers stopped and turned toward John Law. Matt drew the back of his shirtsleeve across his bloody face, then said, "Hell, that where the cells are, right?"

J.T. had torn a rag from a piece of cloth near Abe's desk, and was dabbing at his own bloody face.

"Yeah, but you boys ain't under arrest for anything. not yet anyway." Pointing to two chairs against the wall, J.T. continued. "Have a seat, boys. You want some coffee?"

The boys exchanged curious glances back and forth, then sat down.

"Yeah. I'd like a drink, but not coffee," said Harvey.

"I don't need nothin' to drink" said Matt, "but I could use one of them rags you got there. Only got two shirts and this is my best one."

J.T. tore off another rag and tossed it to Matt. He then reached into Abe's top desk drawer and tossed a half-full bottle of whiskey over to Harvey. Once everyone had gotten halfway cleaned up and settled, the bottle made its way around and back to Harvey.

Matt leaned forward. Resting his elbows on his knees, he continued to dab at his busted lip as he asked, "Just who the hell are you, mister?"

Sitting at Abe's desk, Law replied, "John Thomas Law."

"Goddamn!" sighed Harvey.

Matt agreed with his brother, then said, "Guess it's a damn good thing we didn't try to pull on you. Reckon we'd be dead right now."

"Maybe," said J.T. with a half smile.

Matt laughed, then grimaced from the pain in his face. "Maybe, my ass. Bet that's what them twenty men you put in the graveyard said just before they went for their guns—maybe."

"Since you know we're wanted, you wanta tell us why we ain't settin' in them cells back there?" asked Harvey.

J.T. spun around in his chair and faced the two brothers.

"Because I'm going to make a deal with you boys. But before I do, I'm going to tell you a story, then let you decide what you want to do."

The brothers still looked confused by all this, but nodded and listened intently as J.T. told of the raid on the Covington ranch, leaving nothing out. He described Debbie and Thomas, and said it was a good bet they had seen some, if not all, of the killing that took place that day. He then told the brothers about the plan to go after the children, rescue them from the Comancheros, and bring them back to Texas. By the time he finished, he could see the look of disbelief on the faces of the two men.

Matt shook his head. "You fellas are plumb loco. You go ridin' in there, you'll never ride out. I get the idea you want me an' Harv to go along on this little trip. Well, if that's part of your deal, bounty man, let me tell you somethin'. We might not be the smartest two boys around, but we ain't crazy neither."

Harvey didn't seem to feel that way. He waited until his brother had finished, then asked, "What's your offer of a deal, Law?"

Matt shot an angry look at Harvey. "Don't matter what the deal is, Harv. We ain't gettin' roped into no damn massacre. These fellows wanta get their self killed, let 'em. Ain't no skin off our nose."

Harvey may have been the younger of the two, but he spoke his own mind. "Matt! Shut that damn pie hole of yours for a minute. I wanta hear what the man's got to say."

"It's real simple, Harvey. I believe your story about the two soldiers. Talked to too many people that were there and saw it happen. Clear case of self-defense. But this business with the Ellsworth bank, that ain't gonna go away on its own. You boys are lookin' at twenty-five to thirty years in a Federal prison for that one. Course, if it hadn't been me that caught you, it would have been someone else. Someplace, sometime, a lawman or another bounty hunter would have recognized you boys from one of those flyers, and either shot you down for the reward or been slappin' the chains on. You agree to come along to Mexico with us, and I'll see to it that those flyers are recalled. You won't have to spend the rest of your lives watchin' over your shoulder for lawmen or backshooters. That's it, I reckon. A heap of years in prison or a long ride into Mexico. Choice is up to you, boys."

Matt came out with a smug laugh. "Some deal, huh, Harvey? Grow old in prison or get shot full of holes in a week. You got a real sense of humor there, John T. Law."

Harvey wasn't laughing. The thought of being caged in a four-by-eight cell with nothing to do but pace the floor was his worse nightmare come to life.

"Twenty-five years is a hell of a long time, Matt," said Harvey. "I'd just as soon go down fightin' than rot in a damn prison. At least I'd be free and could die under the open sky, not like some rat in a cage. I'm in, John Thomas Law. When do we leave?"

Matt was on his feet now, yelling at his brother. "You can't do this, Harvey, Goddamnit, I'm the oldest an' I say we ain't goin' in on this."

"Reckon I'm old enough to make up my own mind, Matt. You do what you want. But I'm goin' with these fellas. There's two little kids out there scared to death. They done lost everything. God only knows what's happen to 'em since they been with those Comancheros. I think it's time we done one decent thing in our lives, don't you? Ma would have agreed with me on this and you know it, Matt."

J.T. stood up and walked across the room. He handed Harvey his gunbelt.

"Harvey, I've always believed there were few things a man has in life that's worth much, but a man's word is one of 'em. It's the most important thing he has. It's something that's not given carelessly. Once it has, the people he gives it to have no choice but to honor that vow. It forms a sacred trust between them. I believe you are a man of your word, Harvey. I want to thank you for coming along."

Matt shook his head. "Oh, hell, Harvey. If you're determined to go through with this, I guess I better go along so you don't get your damn head blowed off. Sounds like that'll be a full-time job 'fore this is over. Count me in, bounty man."

Billy brought Matt's holster over to him and grinned. Shaking hands with both men, he said, "Billy Tyler. Glad to know ya."

When Abe returned to the office, he saw all four men bent over the map. Introductions were made all around. Abe didn't bother to ask why the McMasters boys had joined up with them, and J.T. saw no need to explain it. He was just grateful for the help. Abe had gotten the supplies for the trip. The Rangers were busy packing them up as they spoke. They'd be on the trail within the hour.

FIVE

THE TRAIN RIDE to Laredo had seemed long, but not nearly as long as it would have taken them to cover the miles by horseback. Abe hadn't said much during the trip. J.T. knew the loss of his brother and worry about the two kids was occupying his every thought and nothing anyone could say was going to change that. Billy and Harvey had actually begun to form an easy friendship. Although ten years older than Billy, Harvey wasn't much more than a big kid himself. Matt, on the other hand, was still brooding over getting snaked into this deal. He hadn't ever dealt with Comancheros, but from what he'd heard, they were a bad bunch to tangle with. Hell, three men hanging by their heels from a signpost with their ears cut off was pretty damn good testimony to that fact.

J.T. had spent most of the trip familiarizing himself

with the map. It showed a few Mexican villages along the route into the Sierra Madres, but he knew there were a lot more than this map had listed. It was going to be impossible for them to move through the area without drawing the attention of local villagers. Villagers who more than likely were paid by the Comancheros to keep an eye out for strangers. Unless he missed his guess, the leader of the outfit would know that the gringos were in Mexico before they had gone twenty miles. The only thing the Comancheros wouldn't know was who they were and why they were there. John T. was counting on the Comancheros' curiosity about the Americans to help lead them to the enemy camp. As it was now, they had no idea where to start looking for Debbie and Thomas. They couldn't afford to go around asking questions. They didn't know who they could trust. No, they were going to have to wait until someone came looking for them.

It was late at night when the train pulled into the station. The five men unloaded their horses and gear and headed for the livery stable. Getting the horses bedded down, they then went looking for a place for themselves. The Lone Star Hotel was near the general store and mercantile. They got their rooms, and then went to eat at the only restaurant that was open that late at night. The conversation was casual and friendly. A chance for everyone to get to know each other a little better. By the time supper was over, even Abe, being the hard-nosed lawman he was, found himself taking a liking to the McMasters boys. It worked both ways. As they were leaving, J.T. overheard Matt telling his brother, "You know, these fellas ain't bad ol' boys for lawmen." All during supper, no one had talked about the task that lay ahead. There would plenty of time for that once they crossed the border.

As they headed back to the hotel, they heard the music and rowdy laughter coming from the saloons that lined the streets.

"Anybody 'sides me feel like havin' a drink?" asked Matt.

Abe shook his head. "Not me. I gotta put these ol' bones down for the night. You boys go on if you a mind to. Just remember, we got a long day ahead of us tomorrow."

"Don't worry, Abe. I'll see they don't overdo it," said J.T. "You get some sleep. See you in the morning."

Abe nodded and headed off for the hotel, while the others stepped up onto the boardwalk and entered the nearest saloon. The smell of stale beer and cigar smoke was a shock to the nose after having been out in the clean, crisp night air. The bar was packed and there were poker games going on at nearly every table. Billy noticed a group of cowboys getting ready to leave a table along the far wall. Hurrying through the crowd, he quickly claimed it and shouted for one of the waiters, slicing through the crowd with his tray held high, to come over and take their order.

Billy ordered up a pitch of beer. He hadn't ever taken to the hard whiskey. It got him drunk too fast and always left him puking up his guts. Not so with J.T. and the McMasters boys, who asked for a bottle and three glasses. When it arrived, they poured their drinks and took a few minutes to look over the crowd. The place wasn't the fanciest in town, but all of them had drunk in a lot worse. There were six girls working the crowd. None of them looked that young, or if they were, the saloon life had taken a toll on them, making them look older beyond their years. It was the same kind of crowd J.T. had seen in countless saloons all over the West. Cowboys and gamblers, local businessmen and traveling salesmen, all gathered to relax, have a few drinks, and chat with the ladies or try their hand at a game of poker after a long day of punching cows or pushing merchandise.

Matt caught the eye of one of the girls, who came over and began to whisper in his ear. The two laughed. Then Matt downed his drink, winked at the others, and left with the girl to go upstairs, telling them he'd be back down in an hour. Harvey shook his head as he watched his brother take the stairs two at a time.

"Matt's always had a thing for the ladies," he said. "Ma would be rollin' over in her grave if she seen the gals he run around pokin' all the time."

"Your ma's dead?" asked Billy.

"Yeah. Her and Pa both. Me an Matt had run off an' joined the Confederate Army. Matt had just turned twenty. I was seventeen. War was almost over by then. Guess we was afraid we'd miss it if we didn't go then and there. Wish we hadn't now. We both got shot up pretty bad a few weeks 'fore it was all over. Didn't get back home till nearly a year later. By then we found out Pa was killed by some damn Yankees during the occupation after the war. They come to take the place for taxes. Hell, he didn't have no money—nobody in Texas did in them days. But him and Ma had built that place with their own two hands. Lived there near on to thirty years. He wasn't gonna give it up. Run 'em off with an old scattergun. They come back that night, 'bout twenty of 'em, Ma said. Called him out. When Pa walked out onto the porch, they shot him all to pieces. Told Ma she'd get the same if she didn't clear out, then rode off. The no-good sons-a-bitches."

J.T. and Billy could hear the bitterness in Harvey's

voice as he paused and poured himself another drink. J.T. saw the hurt in the man's eyes as Harvey stared at the table. It was a story John Law had heard before from other men in other places. The years following the war had been the darkest days in Texas history. Corrupt politicians, Yankee rules and laws enforced by largely black units of Yankee troopers who went out of their way to remind the Texans that they had lost the war. It had been the cause of a lot of shootings and more than a few hangings.

"What'd your ma do, Harvey?" asked Billy.

Harvey suddenly looked up, smiled, then laughed as he said, "Ma was a tough ol' gal. She buried Pa that night and at first light, she set fire to every damn thing on the place. Burned it all down, by God. The house, the barn, even the damn privy—everything. Tossed the few clothes she had into an old buckboard and left for San Antonio. Took me an' Matt nearly six months to find her. She had been doin' sewin'. Ma was good at such as that, ya know. We found her stayin' in a little storeroom back of one of the saloons. She done sewin' during the day and swept an' cleaned the saloon at night."

Havery's eyes watered up and his voice began to crack to the point he had to stop for a minute. Taking another shot of whiskey, he continued.

"She was mighty sick when we found her. It was late winter and that damn room didn't have no heat, ya see. All she had was some blankets and old feed sacks to keep her warm. She had a real bad cough, and was so weak she could barely get around. But she sure lit up when she saw me an' Matt. She figured we'd got killed in the war. We took out of that pigpen and put her up in a fine hotel. Waited on her like she was the Queen of England, yes, sir. Kept her warm, an' fed her lots of soup and such. Got a doc to come take a look at her. He said she was bad off with pneumonia, but what we was doin' was the best thing for her. After a couple days, she seemed to be gettin' better. Then one mornin', we went in to take her breakfast an' . . . an' she was just gone. Died in her sleep. Me and Matt took her back out to the place. Wasn't nothin' or nobody livin' there. A sign said some Yankee bank owned the land, but hell, we didn't care. We put her on the hill next to Pa overlookin' the place they spent most of their lives buildin'. Didn't see no harm in that. We spent the night on the hill with the folks. Next mornin' we rode off, an' ain't been back since. Guess we started gettin' a little wild after that."

Billy slumped back in his chair. J.T. could see the water forming in the young Ranger's eyes. It was a sad story, no doubt about that. One that had been repeated over and over all too often in Texas. Sipping his whiskey, he looked over at Harvey.

"All this have anything to do with that bank in Ellsworth, Kansas?"

Harvey nodded. "Yeah. Hell, we never robbed no damn bank before. Won't have robbed that one neither if it hadn't been for the name on the place. Same bunch of Northern sons-a-bitches that take our place owned that bank. Me and Matt saw that, well, guess we just got a little crazy. We was ridin' out of town. Saw the sign, stopped them horses dead in the middle of the street, then looked at each other. Wasn't a word passed between us. Just got off our horses, walked in, and robbed the damn place. Just seemed like the thing to do at the time."

Having listened to Harvey's story, Billy Tyler found it hard not to agree with the outlaw. Hell, he wasn't so sure he wouldn't have done the same thing. J.T. didn't have

to think about it. He had done the same thing with the
James boys.

Harvey poured another drink and looking at his two
new friends, said, "I'd appreciate it if ya'll would kinda
keep all that stuff to yourself. Matt, he's always sayin' I
talk too much. He wouldn't take too kindly me talkin'
about private family business."

J.T. and Billy both nodded. Harvey was about to say
something else when he suddenly set his glass down and
stared hard at a man who had just come in the front doors.

"Well, I'll be damned. If my eyes ain't failin' me, that
fellow there is Shotgun Pete Simmons. Met him in a poker
game in Dodge City. We spent a few days drinkin', gam-
blin', and raisin' hell. Little rough around the edges, but
a damn likable fellow once ya get to know him. Use to
ride with Texas Jack Collins and Dutch Henry Brown up
in the Oklahoma Territory. Man was good with a shooter
or a rifle, but preferred the solid kick of a scattergun when
he was in a fight. Saw him make that backshootin' bastard
Jim Miller crawdad last summer up in Waco. Man ain't
afraid of nothin' that walks, flies, or crawls. Last I heard,
he was in irons an' on his way to Judge Parker's court at
Fort Smith. Figured that ol' hangin' judge had stretched
his neck by now."

This sounded like the kind of man J.T. was looking for,
but from what he could see, Pete Simmons appeared about
as down on his luck as any one man could be. His clothes
were filthy, his hair matted and tangled, and his face
looked like it hadn't seen water in a mouth. Even the men
at the bar moved downwind of him as he stepped up to
order a drink. Sliding his chair back, J.T. said, "Don't
appear that Ol' Man Parker got the job done. Think I'll
see if Shotgun would like to join us for a drink."

As John Thomas neared the bar, a terrible, but familiar, odor filled his nostrils. It was a combination of sweat, vomit, and shit all mixed together. It was clear by sight and smell that Pete hadn't had a bath in a month of Sundays and that the clothes he wore more than likely were the only ones he had. J.T. figured him to be in his fifties. His dirt-crusted fingers were wrapped tight around the shot glass of whiskey. He was nursing that one drink as if it were the last one in the world. Braving the elements, J.T. stepped up to the bar next to him and ordered a bottle of whiskey. Pete didn't even take notice. When the bottle arrived, J.T. poured himself a drink and leaning against the bar, looked over at the man.

"You're Shotgun Pete Simmons, ain't you?"

Simmons glanced over at Law. His eyes were red and bloodshot. Heavy bags under his eyes bore testament to too much booze and little sleep. The dirt helped conceal wrinkled lines that ran through his weatherworn, leathery face. A face that had once been strong and threatening, now lost in a whirling fog of alcohol and confusion. It was a face John Thomas had seen before in a mirror.

Turning back to his shot glass, Pete muttered, "Go away, boy. Ya got me mixed up with somebody else."

Law took a sip of his whiskey. "Oh, I don't think so. I think you're the same Shotgun Pete that used to ride with Dutch Henry Brown."

Simmons didn't bother to look up.

"How about Texas Jack Collins?"

This name got a reaction. Pete stood upright, grabbed Law's vest, and met J.T.'s eyes with a cold hard stare. "That son of a bitch! What d'ya know about Jack? Where is that no-good bastard? I'm gonna gut him—then blow his goddamn head off! Where is he?"

J.T. gripped the man's wrist tight and removed it from his vest.

"Easy, Pete. He's standin' trial up in Denison, Texas. They figure to hang him in a couple of weeks."

A smile appeared through the dirty face at the welcome news. Pete backed off, nodded his approval, then turned back to his drink. Raising it high, he laughed, then downed it in one swift gulp. Placing the glass back on the bar, Pete turned to leave. J.T. reached out and grabbed his arm.

"Pete. My friends and I would like you to join us for a drink. That is, if you've got the time."

Pete eased his arm out of Law's grip and looked at him long and hard before saying, "I swear, mister. I got no idea who ya are. How ya know me anyway?"

"Harvey McMasters. He saw you come in."

The old man's eyes seemed to brighten at the mention of the name.

"Matt and Harvey McMasters?" he asked.

"That's right. Matt's upstairs gettin' his rope pulled, but Harvey's at the table with us. Come on over, Pete."

Pete hesitated for a moment, but then followed J.T. over to the table. Harvey got to his feet and reached out his hand, trying hard not to ignore the odor.

"Hey, Pete. How the hell ya been?"

"Been gettin' by, boy. That's about all we can do, I reckon."

"Well, have a seat."

Pete pulled up a chair, ignoring the looks he was getting from the people around them. Harvey poured him a drink as he said, "Pete, that youngster on your right there is Billy Tyler. The fellow across from ya is J.T. Law."

Pete's hand suddenly reached down, but then he remembered he didn't have a gun anymore. He'd traded it for a bottle of whiskey somewhere along the line.

"Jesus, boy!" said Pete, "Don't ya know who this fellow is? He's a damn man-hunter."

"Easy, Pete," said J.T. "We're all friends here. Harvey and Matt are working on something with me. Nobody's out to put anybody in jail, okay? Relax."

Harvey couldn't stand it any longer. He had to ask. "Damn, Pete, what the hell happen to ya? Ya look like somethin' the cat dragged in."

"Yeah," said Billy, keeping his glass of whiskey near his nose to ward off the smell. "Somethin' dead at that."

Pete didn't take offense. Instead, he downed his drink, then filled his glass again.

"Harvey thought you were due up at Judge Parker's court at Fort Smith, Pete. That right?" asked John Thomas.

Pete downed his whiskey as if it were water.

"Yeah, I was 'pose to be there, all right. Marshal had me in that damn prison wagon of his for near on a week. Wouldn'a been there neither if it hadn't been for that damn no-good Texas Jack. Him and that son of a bitch Dutch Brown ran out on me when a posse cornered us. Left me to fight them boys by myself. The posse shot my horse, and them boys didn't wanta carry double, so they just lit out on me. Hope them folks in Denison hang that bastard slow. I'll deal with Dutch when I see him next, ya can count on that."

"You won't get the chance, Pete," said Billy.

The old man shot him a look. "What ya talkin' 'bout, boy?"

"J.T. here shot him dead little over a week ago. He's also the one that caught Texas Jack and brought him in."

Pete directed his attention to J.T., looking at him with red, untrusting eyes.

"Ya killed Dutch and hogtied Texas Jack, yet yer a-sittin' here with me and Harvey, with Matt upstairs. Yer knownin' we're all wanted men, an ya ain't lookin' to collect no bounty on any of us. That right?"

J.T. grinned. "That's right, Pete. Me and the McMasters boys got a deal. I was hopin' maybe we could count you in on it too."

Pete shook his head, trying to figure this out, but no matter how many ways he studied it, it didn't come out right somehow.

"Damn if I know what yer game is, J.T. Law, but I'm obliged to ya for what ya done to Dutch Henry and that son-of-a-bitchin' Texas Jack. I figure yer wonderin' how I got away from that Oklahoma marshal, ain't ya?"

"Thought did cross my mind," said John T.

Pete took another drink and then told his story. They had picked up a few more prisoners on the way to Fort Smith. The prison wagon was nearly full. He overheard the marshal saying they had one more stop to make, in a place called Choctaw, to pick up a couple of whiskey runners. Pete knew something was wrong the minute they pulled into town. There wasn't a soul on the street. They pulled up in front of the sheriff's office and the marshal went inside. There wasn't anyone there. As he was coming out, three men opened fire on the lawman from the rooftops across the street. Must have hit him eight or nine times. They cut down the driver when he leaped off the wagon and made a break for the sheriff's office. Before Pete and the others knew what happened, some breed jumped on the wagon and whipped the horses out of town.

They went three or four miles before the man stopped

the rig. Four other half-bloods rode up a little later. Pete said he could tell by the look of them that they were a mean bunch. They talked about what they should do with the prisoners. Then three more fellas showed up. Two of them were white men. From what Pete could tell, they were the ones the sheriff had been holding for the marshal. The breeds had killed the sheriff and terrorized the town, then decided to ambush the marshal when he arrived. A couple of them wanted to shoot all the prisoners while they were still in the cage. But the leader, a damn big buck with long black hair and a headband, said no to that idea. He figured all those in that wagon were wanted men. That meant bounty money. But they couldn't turn them all in at the same time or in the same place. They decided to split them up like so many head of cattle.

There were eight of them and eight prisoners. They split up into two groups. Four of them took four of the prisoners with them and headed toward Tulsa. They figured to turn in two there and two along the way. Pete and three other prisoners went along with the lead buck, who was headed for Muskogee. The prisoners were kept in chains and were led on foot, with ropes around their necks, behind the horses. One man couldn't keep up the pace. When he fell, they kept dragging him along behind them. Pete said the other prisoners yelled at the men to stop, that they were choking the man to death, but the men only laughed and said bounties would be paid for the prisoners dead or alive. The dragged prisoner choked to death. After three or four miles, the men finally stopped, threw his body over one of the horses, and started off again.

Just before dark, they stopped by a river and set up camp. The prisoners were sent out under the watchful eye of a breed with a rifle to gather wood for the fire. The other two men with Pete saw him pick up a solid limb he could use for a club, and they did the same. Nothing was said between them. There was no need for words. After seeing what the men had done earlier, the prisoners didn't figure they had much to lose. Maybe one of them would get away, but no matter, getting shot was better than being slowly strangled while being dragged behind a damn horse.

Moving back into camp, the prisoners had a few things going for them. It was getting darker by the minute and the fire was barely giving off any light. Three of the breeds were standing together around the fire, their rifles lying across their saddles on the ground. The only real immediate threat was the man behind the prisoners with the rifle. They were only going to get one chance. As they bent down to drop their load of wood, each prisoner came back up suddenly with a tree limb in his hands and bashed the men around the fire. There were screams of pain, cussing, and total confusion for the next few seconds.

One of the prisoners ran for the horses. The man guarding the prisoners fired two shots at him, the second one finding its mark and dropping the prisoner a few feet short of the picket line. The other prisoner ran from the camp and dove into some thick brush. At the same time, Pete leaped into the river, the current taking him under and carrying him downstream. When he came up for air, he could hear shots being fired, but none were coming his way. He didn't know if they got the other prisoner or not. He didn't think so, because he could still hear the firing going on the farther he got downstream. He caught onto a log and rode it maybe five or six miles downriver before he felt it was safe to swim to shore.

He walked for days without seeing a soul. Then, on the

fourth day, he came across an old black man and his Cherokee wife. They had a soddy near a stream. When she saw Pete's chains, she got frightened and ran into the house. The old man didn't say a word, simply waved Pete over to an anvil and broke the chains off with a hammer and a chisel. He said he knew what it was like to wear chains and he wouldn't abide by it, no matter what Pete had done to warrant such treatment. They fed him, then sent him on his way with some jerky and biscuits.

After walking another three days, Pete admitted to stealing a horse from a farm near the Red River. He couldn't walk anymore. It wasn't till he had gone twenty miles that he realized the horse was blind in one eye, but it managed to get him as far as San Antonio before it gave out on him. He sold it for a few dollars and kept moving south, trying to put as much distance between him and that dead marshal as possible. He ended up in Laredo, bought five bottles of whiskey, and camped out down by the Rio. He no money, no gun, and no horse. He was flat busted with nothing to do and nowhere to go. So he just stayed drunk for nearly a week. This had been the first time he'd been in Laredo since. He had panhandled the little bit of change he'd used to buy the shot at the bar. Finished with his story, Pete sat back in his chair.

"That's it, boys. I just hope some of them other fellows got away too."

"I got one question, Mr. Simmons," said Billy.

"What's that, son?"

"How can a man camp right on the banks of the Rio Grande and not get a damn drop of water on him?"

Pete saw Harvey and J.T. grin. Then he looked at the dirt crusted on his hands.

"Well, sonny. After nearly drownin' in one river sober,

guess I was downright afraid of gettin' in another one when I was shitface drunk. But I can see what ya mean. I done let my appearance go a little longer than most folks, I reckon. Hell, a drunk can't smell nothing. Do it smell bad?"

"It do," said Billy.

J.T. and Harvey both quickly agreed with Tyler, then laughed as Pete pulled the front of his shirt up to his nose and sniffed. The expression on his face said it all.

"My Lord. It's a wonder somebody ain't done shot me for smellin' that bad. My apologies, boys. But don't really matter, I reckon. These here rags is all I got to my name right now."

"How'd you like to change that, Pete?" asked J.T.

"Ya done got my attention, bounty man."

J.T. told Pete the same story he had told Matt and Harvey. When he finished, he and the others waited to see what Pete had to say.

The old outlaw was surprised. He had been in a stupor when he walked in the saloon, but now, sitting here, he was drinking and thinking clearer than he had in a week. Maybe it was the company and the conversation, or the fact that he was drinking with the man that had put Texas Jack's neck in a hangman's rope. He wasn't sure which. But whatever it was, he felt that maybe his luck had changed. After the last couple of weeks he'd had, fighting a bunch of Comancheros was nothing.

Looking across the table at J.T., he said, "Son, I told ya up front I ain't got nothin' but these here ol' rags on my smelly ass. No gun, no horse, no clothes, no saddle, an' no money. How am I gonna do ya any good even if I wanted to?"

"We got a deal?" asked J.T.

"Well, I reckon so. Ain't doin' nothin' else right now. But I ain't walkin' behind no more horses."

J.T. pulled a small leather bag out of his coat pocket and tossed it across the table. It landed in front of Pete, who opened it and looking inside, saw more gold coins than he'd seen in years.

"You hang on to that," said J.T. "First thing tomorrow, get yourself cleaned up and outfitted with whatever you're gonna need for the trip. Guns, saddle, horse, everything. Pay for it all out of that money and give me back whatever's left."

Pete couldn't believe it. "Ya sayin' yer gonna trust me with this here money of yers?"

J.T. stood up. Finishing his drink, he walked by Pete and put his hand on the old man's shoulder. "Pete, I figure any fellow that can make Deacon Jim Miller back down in a fight is a man I can trust all day long. I'll see you boys in the morning."

Pete watched the gunfighter walk away. Looking over at Harvey and Billy, he said, "That boy's a right likable fellow. Hear tell he's killed over twenty men."

"Twenty-two," said Billy. "Be a lot more 'fore this thing's over."

Pete tossed the bag of coins up and down in his hand. "Damn, I sure hate to wait till mornin' to get this stink off me."

The men at the poker table next to them stopped playing and looked over at Pete. One of the cowboys spoke for the others.

"We do too, ol'-timer. There's a Chinaman at the end of the street runs a bath and steam house. He's open all night. You might wanta pay him a visit tonight."

Pete frowned. He wasn't use to people telling him what

to do. But then again, after smelling himself, he couldn't blame folks for offering advice.

"Thanks, young fella. I think I'd do just that."

Finishing his drink, Pete stood up. Looking at Billy and Harvey, he asked, "Ya boys wanta come along?"

Both men declined. Reaching into his vest pocket, Billy tossed Pete a key.

"What's this?" Pete asked.

"Key to my room. Lone Star Hotel. Number 9 upstairs. We're about the same size. Ya'll find a couple of shirts and two pairs of pants in the saddlebags. Take what ya need. No store open till tomorrow. Ya'll need some clean clothes after your bath."

Pete Simmons was a hard man who had been around a long time, and not one given to emotion, but Billy's offer humbled him. He knew he couldn't speak at the moment, so he merely nodded and walked away. No one in the place noticed the tears welling up in his old bloodshot eyes as he left.

SIX

✦

AS MORNING BROKE across the mountains of the Sierras, a lone rider made his way through narrow canyon passageways and passed the sentries stationed at various points along the route that led to the Devil's Den. The end of the canyon opened out into a scenic valley of trees and streams, with a huge waterfall that got its water from an underground cavern. Set in the middle of this hidden paradise was the headquarters for Bill Purvis and his band of renegade Comancheros.

"Rider comin' in!" shouted one of the guards stationed at the gate. The word was passed on until it reached the men standing on the front porch of the main house. Bill, Pablo, and Mitch Lee all came outside and watched as the rider approached.

"Bet that fellow's carryin' word about your rifles," said Lee.

" 'Bout damn time," answered Purvis.

"*Sí,*" said Pablo. "I'm tired of sitting around here. I need some excitement."

The rider pulled up in front of the house. Taking a message from his shirt pocket, he swung down out of the saddle, hurried up the steps, and gave it to Purvis. The big man read the note, then smiled.

"Well, ya don't got to be bored no more, Pablo. Get the boys ready to ride."

Pablo grinned and ran down the steps and toward the bunkhouse with the excitement of a kid knowing he was going to a candy store.

"How many guards?" asked Lee.

"Twenty-five cavalrymen with five wagons carryin' rifles and ammunition. They'll be moving through Casa Blanco Pass sometime around noon. That's about ten miles across the Rio. We'll hit 'em there. Grab the wagons and head back here."

"Sounds easy enough. Pablo gonna head up the party again?"

"No. I think I'll be leadin' this one. Don't want nothin' goin' wrong. Them rifles are too important to this deal. I want ya and Frank to head out ahead of us. Get to the pass and find us a good spot for the ambush. We won't be far behind ya."

Lee nodded and left to find Frank Taggart, while Purvis looked back down at the message. His man in Laredo had added a postscript. "This information worth more than I am being paid. Will expect addition thousand dollars for more information in the future."

Purvis crumpled the paper tightly in his fist. This was

the second time his mystery informant had raised the price on him. If he tried it once more, the man wasn't going to have a future. Tossing the paper to the ground, he went inside, and returned to the porch with his guns, two cross-belted Colt. 45's. Strapping them on as he walked across the compound, he moved to the cage where Debbie and Thomas were being held. The boy clung tightly to his sister as Purvis approached and knelt down in front of them.

"How ya kids doin'?" he asked.

Thomas hid his face behind his sister. Debbie didn't look away. There was a defiant look in her eyes as she stared at Purvis.

"You're gonna wish you'd never took us when my uncle finds out what you did."

Purvis laughed. "Oh, is that right. An' just who might this all-important uncle of yers be?"

"Captain Abe Covington. He's a Texas Ranger and he's got a whole company of Rangers that work for him. Wouldn't be surprised if they wasn't on their way here right now to kill all of you."

"Oh, so he's a Ranger, is he," said Bill with a sly grin. "Well, little girl, me and my boys here, we eat Texas Rangers for breakfast. They come ridin' in here, they'll end up just like your folks. So if'n I was you, I'd be hopin' he stayed in Texas."

Debbie had caught a glimpse of concern in the big man's eyes when she had mentioned the Texas Rangers. "You don't know my uncle, mister. He ain't afraid of nothin'. He'd chase the devil himself all the way to Hades with a bucket of water if he had a need to. He's comin', all right. You can count on that. You're the one that oughta be hopin' he stays in Texas."

Purvis laughed again. He had to give her credit. This
little blond-haired gal with the sparkling blue eyes wasn't
short on nerve, and he liked that. It showed strong char-
acter for someone her age.

"Little lady, ya just take care of yer brother there and
let me do the worryin' 'bout yer uncle. I gotta go away
for a while, but the womenfolk'll take care of ya while
I'm gone. Ya need anything, ya let 'em know. We'll talk
again when I get back."

Debbie watched the man walk away. She kept the defiant look on her face just in case he happened to look
back at her. But once he was out of sight, she sighed and
leaned back against the cage. Tears began to well up in
her eyes. She wanted to believe that Uncle Abe would
come to save them, but the man was right. There were so
many of them that surely he would be killed if he did
come. She had already seen so many of her family die.
She couldn't bear to see it happen again.

Lee and Taggart had found the perfect spot to set up
the ambush. In order to get to Laredo, the soldiers had
two options. One, go around the mountain, which would
add another day to their trip. Two, utilize the Casa Blanco
Pass, a natural rock formation that had formed at the base
of the mountains. It was narrow at the opening, but widened out after a hundred yards and ran all the way through
the mountains. Lee and Taggart both had been in the military and knew that after two days and nights in the saddle, the last thing a cavalryman wanted was to add another
day to his saddle-worn ass. They'd take the shortcut, no
doubt about that.

While Lee watched to the northwest for any sign of the

Army, Frank rode back toward the Rio and linked up with Purvis and the Comancheros. Big Bill agreed with their choice of sites, and the group followed Taggart back to where Lee was waiting. Once there, Purvis told Frank to take half the men up in the rocks on the left, and Pablo to put his bunch up on the right. Purvis would fire the first shot. He emphasized that no one was to fire until he did. He wanted to be sure he had the soldiers all in the open before the killing started. There would be no survivors. Purvis then climbed the mountain and dropped down beside Mitch Lee.

"Anything yet?" Purvis asked.

Lee passed him the glasses. "Got a dust cloud about three miles out to the northwest. That could be them."

Purvis stared long and hard through the binoculars. Lowering them, he removed his watch from his vest pocket. It was ten minutes till noon. With a short laugh and a grin, he said, "That's what I like about them Yankee soldiers. They surely do set a lot of store by keepin' a schedule. Go signal the boys that they're comin'."

The sweltering sun hung over the troopers, the temperature hovering near a hundred. Purvis kept checking their progress through the glasses. It seemed as through they were hardly moving as minutes stretched into a half hour, then an hour. Speaking through dry lips, Lee said, "So much for stayin' on a damn schedule."

"It's those wagons that's holdin' 'em back. Guns and bullets got a lot of weight to 'em, makes for slow goin' in that damn sand. But they're gettin' here, that's all that matters."

Thirty minutes later, the soldiers came to a stop a half mile from the entrance to the pass. Watching through his glasses, Purvis saw the two men out front appeared to be in a heated discussion. They both appeared to be officers. One kept pointing to the east, the long way around the mountain. The other was shaking his head and pointing to the opening into the pass. Damn, thought Purvis, what if they did decide to go around? Even though the comancheros outnumbered the Yankee cavalry, he had no desire to take them on in a fight out in the open. He might not care much for Yankee troopers, but he had to give them their due. They were damn good shots with a rifle, and with those wagons to use for cover, they could make a stand and hold their ground. But he had to have those rifles. It might cost him a lot of his men, but it was the wagons that were important. He could always get more men.

He was worried for nothing. The man who wanted to take the pass pulled a watch from his pocket and held it up in front of the other officer. Purvis smiled to himself. "That's right, Cap'n, you're behind schedule."

Within minutes, the troopers were passing below Lee and Purvis and into a waiting nightmare. Big Bill gave Lee the glasses, and hurried back down from the crest of the ridge to a spot where he had placed his rifle. Taking up a position, he leveled the Winchester down toward the valley floor and sighted in on the officer with the watch. Purvis waited until he saw the last two troopers trailing the fifth wagon come into sight. The Comancheros now had all of the troopers in plain sight. When the shooting started, the troopers would find themselves caught in a deadly crossfire. Lee dropped down next to Purvis. Levering a round into his rifle, Bill asked, "Ya to start the ball?"

"Start the music, Bill," replied Lee as he sighted in on the back of a trooper.

Purvis fired, the crack of the rifle echoing along the canyon walls. The lead officer tumbled from his horse. Suddenly, the valley canyon was filled with the thundering sound of over thirty rifles spitting death at the valley floor. Over half of the troopers were killed in the initial volley. Others, wounded but hanging onto their saddles, managed to make it to the relative safety of the wagons. Bullets were hitting all around them. Stunned at first, the soldiers, all veterans, quickly regained their composure and began to return fire at their tormentors hidden among the rocks on both sides of them. Horses screamed and reared up as they were hit repeatedly by rifle fire, until finally they fell over onto their sides and died. Purvis was determined that not a single trooper would escape with his life from the canyon.

Pablo Chacon was firing as fast as he could, as if he were afraid the action might end too soon. Reloading, he sighted in on a trooper who had been hit twice and knocked from his horse. He was trying to crawl to the safety of the wagons. Chacon shouted to one of his comrades.

"Twenty dollars I can hit that one in the head!"

"Yer on, Pablo. Double if I get him first?"

Pablo nodded that they had a bet. Sighting in on the wounded man, Chacon slowly squeezed the trigger. The bullet clipped the trooper's left ear and went into the sand.

"Aw, too bad, amigo. My turn."

The other man fired, missing and kicking sand into the soldier's eyes.

Chaon quickly brought his rifle up again, a determined look on his face. He was not a man who liked to lose. He fired, and the back of the soldier's head exploded like a ripe melon. Amid the thundering rifle fire, the faint laughter of two men could be heard in the valley.

As the battle continued, Purvis began to take notice of how many of his men were suddenly being hit. He saw three pitch forward and fall down the side of the mountain on Pablo's side of the canyon. Below, he saw two more of his men jerk upright and tumble amid the rocks. Mitch Lee pointed out three more lying dead near the canyon floor. How in the hell was that possible? Lee quickly pointed to the wagons.

"Those boys ain't dumb. You see how they all gathered around those two wagons in the rear?"

Purvis peered over the rock he was hiding behind. "Yeah, What about it?"

"Nobody's firing at those two. See the markings? They're the ammunition wagons. Frank and Pablo have figured that out already. They won't fire at them boys over there for fear of blowin' that ammunition all to hell."

Purvis hadn't thought about that. He saw three shots kick the sand around one of those wagons. The shots had come from one of his men a few feet below him.

"Goddamnit! Don't be shootin' at them wagons, ya idiot. They're loaded with ammunition. Pass it on!" shouted Purvis.

Looking at Lee, Purvis asked, "Now what the hell we gonna do?"

Lee watched the action for a moment. He was counting bodies. Out of the twenty-five troopers that had ridden into the canyon, seventeen lay dead in the sand. The remainder had gathered under and around the ammo wagons, and were laying down a lethal barrage of rifle fire themselves.

Mitch Lee lit what was left of an earlier cigar and took a deep drag on it before he answered. "I'll take six men down with me and flank 'em. When Frank sees what I'm doin', he'll do the same. We'll box 'em in. See if we can't take 'em down by shootin' low. You all keep firin' just to keep 'em honest."

Purvis nodded. "Sounds good to me, Mitch. Pick yer men."

As he moved down the side of the ridge, Lee saw Dog firing his rifle from the rocks. Next to him lay his bow and a quiver of arrows. He shouted for the breed to bring the bow and arrows and join him, and the two men made their way down the ridge, picking up a man here and there along the way. From across the canyon, Frank Taggart saw what his longtime partner was trying to do, and quickly followed suit.

Instructing his men to keep their firing low, Lee sent Dog with his bow and arrows around to take up a position to the rear of the wagons. Two soldiers had leaped into the back of the last wagon, and were laying down a deadly barrage of rifle fire from inside. For the moment, that was the safest place to be. The two troopers had quickly realized that the Comancheros had restricted their fire toward the ammo wagons for fear of blowing them up. What they hadn't counted on was a half-breed Comanche who had been trained in the use of a bow and arrow since he was old enough to walk.

Low-crawling to within thirty yards of the last wagon, Dog carefully placed an arrow in place. The soldiers hadn't seen him yet. When they paused to reload, the breed came up on his knees and drew the bow back as far as it would go. The arrow sliced through the air and into the back of one of the soldiers. As the man fell forward, the other trooper in the wagon saw Dog jump to his feet and notch another arrow onto the bow. Letting out a bloodcurdling Comanche yell, Dog began running as fast as he could toward the rear of the wagon. The yell had made the trooper's blood run cold as he desperately brought up his rifle and fired off two shots at the charging figure. Both shots missed. Ignoring the bullets that missed his head by inches, Dog drew back the bow and sent the arrow on a true path, straight into the soldier's heart.

Leaping into the back of the wagon, Dog pulled his knife and cut the throats of both men just to make sure they were dead. Moving to a position behind the springboard seat, he put another arrow into the throat of another trooper firing from the rear of the wagon in front of him. As Lee and Taggart pressed their attacks on the remaining soldiers, other troopers went down. Finally, in desperation, one of the remaining two troopers crawled forward and managed to cut one of the leaders free from its harness. Leaping onto the back of the horse, he called to his wounded comrade and held out his hand to swing the man up behind him onto the horse. It was a valiant effort, but one that was not to be. As the wounded trooper reached up to his friend, three bullets struck him in the back and he fell dead.

The mounted trooper, now the sole survivor, was hit by a bullet in the shoulder, the impact nearly knocking him off the horse. But the man's desire to live caused his hand to shoot out and grab a handful of the horse's mane as he held on and kicked the animal in the ribs. The horse leaped forward and began to run for the entrance into the canyon. Every rifle in the pass was firing at him, but for a brief moment, it almost looked like he might make it out of this canyon of death. Mitch Lee, Purvis, and Pablo Chacon all sighted in on the single rider and fired virtually at the same time. The three bullets found their targets.

One struck the horse. Its front legs suddenly collapsed, sending the rider flying over its head and into the sand. But it didn't matter. The other two shots had hit him in the head and the back. The trooper had been dead before he ever hit the ground.

A sudden silence hung over the canyon floor. The only sound was the low whistling of the wind as it blew through the opening between the canyon walls. Everything seemed to come to a complete halt as the victors surveyed their handiwork. The bodies of dead troopers and horses littered the sand. Finally, Purvis and the others began to make their way down from the rocks and toward the wagon.

Frank Taggart walked to the back of the last wagon. Pulling the canvas back to look inside, he found Dog, one hand holding the head of a soldier up by the hair while with the other, he sawed away at one of the man's ears with a knife. The breed paused in his task long enough to look back at Taggart and grin, before continuing with his grisly work. Unknown to the Indian, Taggart's hand had dropped down to the grip of his .45. For a fleeting second, the gunman considered killing the depraved son of a bitch right then and there. There was no call for this kind of savagery. The troopers had fought a courageous battle to the very end against overwhelming odds. It was enough that they were dead. In Taggart's mind, they were due a measure of respect. Not being cut up like pigs at a slaughterhouse. Taggart's gun was halfway out of the holster when Mitch Lee walked up next to him. Looking inside, he reached over, and placed his hand over Taggart's gun hand, and pulling his friend away from the wagon, said, "Forget it, Frank. We got work to do."

As they walked away, Taggart pulled his arm free.

"That ain't right, Mitch, an' you know it. Maybe it's time we pulled outta this outfit. I mean, here we are kidnappin' little kids and cuttin' ears off brave men. I know I ain't no fuckin' saint, Mitch, but I'd like to think I still got a little honor left. There ain't no honor in what we just saw back there, that's for damn sure. What'd you say?"

Lee shook his head. "Not a good time, Frank. There's gonna be plenty of money and gold come from all these here rifles and ammunition. We leave now, we're out our share. Forget about Dog. Somebody's gonna end up killing the crazy bastard one of these days anyway."

Frank wouldn't argue that point. If the breed wasn't dead when Frank decided to pull out, he would be before he left. Frank Taggart was going to make sure of that.

Purvis was shouting orders for the cut harness to be fixed and another horse to be brought up to replace the one killed. It was clear from the gruff sound of his voice that the Comanchero leader was aggravated. He'd lost eight men in this fight, and he wasn't happy about it. He kept trying to figure out who to blame for it, but there wasn't anyone really. The cavalrymen had simply put up one hell of a good fight. Who was to blame for that?

Within the hour, they were on the move with the wagons and headed back toward the Rio. Dog rode up and down the line a few times before he took the point, making sure everyone had an opportunity to see the new collection of ears that he had collected. He had them strung on a piece of wire that hung from his saddlehorn. Few of the Comancheros took notice. They'd grown accustomed to the breed's sick sense of humor and crazy antics. Nothing the man did surprised them anymore.

Purvis had hoped to have his loot safely back at the

Devil's Den just after dark, but that plan went astray a few miles after they had crossed the Rio. One of the ammunition wagons dropped into a hole and shattered the spokes in one of the wheels. There wasn't room in the other wagon to off-load the boxes, but even if there were, it would have been too heavy a load. There was little they could do but find another wagon. After talking it over among themselves, it was decided that Chacon, Taggart, and Lee, with three other men, would go into the nearest town and get another wagon, while another six of the men remained to guard the ammunition. Purvis would take the other four wagons and the rest of the men on to the Devil's Den. This arrangement was fine with Chacon. It would give them a chance to visit a few of the cantinas before they headed back to the mountain fortress.

IN LAREDO, J.T. and Abe had been up since daylight. Over breakfast, Law told the Ranger about his meeting with Shotgun Pete Simmons. Abe recognized the name, but was surprised to hear the old hard case was still alive. Rumor had it he'd been killed up in the Nations by a posse. J.T. assured Covington that the man was very much alive and willing to join them on their trip across the Rio. That made six. Not much of a force to go up against an army, but with a little luck and some good planning, they just might be able to get those two kids out of there and back home to Texas. Of course, no one had seen Pete since he had left the saloon last night to visit the Chinaman's bathhouse. Billy and the McMasters boys thought maybe John T. had seen the last of his money, and said so. J.T., on the other hand, didn't appear to be bothered by their talk, vowing that Pete would be there when they were ready to ride.

Following breakfast, the men packed their gear and went to the livery to saddle their horses while they waited for Abe and J.T. to pick up the supplies they would need for their trek into the mountains of Mexico. Matt had been given the task of picking out two pack mules to carry the load. It became clear to the livery owner early on that Matt McMasters didn't know a thing about mules, especially pack mules, and like any good businessman he saw an opportunity to rid himself of two of the most troublesome animals he had in the corral.

With Harvey and Tyler looking on, Matt followed the owner over to where two mules were standing alone in a corner of the corral.

"Yes, sir, sonny. These here two mules are the best of the bunch. Got'um for a local prospector that worked the hills around here. He gave it up an' went back East a month ago. They can carry damn near any size load anywhere you got a mind to go."

To Matt, they just looked like two dumb-ass mules. But with the others watching, he had to at least act like he knew what he doing. He reached out and ran his hand down the back of one of the mules, squeezed a leg here and there. Next, he walked to the front of the mule and tried to check the animal's teeth, as if he were buying a horse. The mule nearly took his fingers off.

"That's all right, son. They're just a little skittish since their owner's been gone. They'll get used to you by the time you're ready to leave," said the liveryman with a reassuring smile.

Matt started to move around to the other side of the mule, but the owner quickly took him by the arm and pulled him back to the left side of the animal.

"Looky there at them legs. I tell you, son, this critter could walk to Saint Louie totin' a carriage on his back without even breathin' hard. An' that there other one is even younger and stronger than this one. No, sir, boy. You ain't gonna find a better set of mules in this whole county. So what's you say? They're worth at least a hundred for the pair, but since I like you, son, I'll let you have 'em for forty dollars apiece."

Matt nodded. "Sounds fair enough to me."

Reaching into his pocket, he pulled out some money and began counting it out. Just as he was about to hand the forty dollars over, a voice from the stable called out.

"I'd be holdin' on to that there money if'n I was you, boy."

Matt and the liveryman looked across the corral at the man sitting a handsome mare with a blaze face and three white-stocking feet. The man sat ramrod-straight, and there was a shotgun lying across his saddle. Billy elbowed Harvey in the ribs.

"Well, I'll be damned. Would ya look at that. That's ol' Pete."

Harvey didn't believe it at first. No way this could be that smelly old dirt-faced man with the scraggly beard that had been drinking with them at their table last night. Taking a step closer, Harvey eyed the new clothes, the hat, and the new boots. The dirt and grime were gone from the face, as was the beard. But the eyes told the story.

"By God, Billy, yer right as rain. That's Pete Simmons, sure enough."

As he stepped down from his horse, Harvey and Billy saw the new holster and gunbelt strapped around the old man's waist. Pete Simmons was a Smith & Wesson man.

He was carrying a Schofield single-action .45. But the item that really drew their attention was the shotgun. It was a brand-new ten-gauge double-barrel that had been cut down.

He joined his young cohorts, and the three men walked through the gate and across the corral to where dealing for the mules was taking place. Billy made the introductions.

"Matt. This here is Shotgun Pete Simmons, the fellow we were tellin' ya about this morning. Pete, this is Matt McMasters, Harvey's older brother."

Matt reached out and shook Pete's hand as he said, "Ya sayin' there's somethin' wrong with these here mules?"

Pete didn't answer. Moving to the first of the pair of mules, he walked around the animal. He stopped on the far side of the first mule and knelt down at the rear right leg. Just above the hoof on the inside was an open sore.

"This mule's got an abscess. Doubt he'd make it as far as the Rio."

Standing up, Pete shot the liveryman a knowing look as he moved to the other animal. Pete placed his hand on its head and moved the hand slowly down to the end of the nose. He then took a quick step to the left, then back again. Matt and the others watched with curiosity. Not one of them had any idea what Pete was doing. Turning to the owner, Pete stared him straight in the eyes.

"So ya say these is prime mules, do ya, Mr. Livery Man?"

It was plain that the man was getting nervous. "Well . . . yeah. But I didn't know that leg had gone bad. Got it stuck 'tween some slats few days ago. Figured it'd be all right. But there ain't nothin' wrong with that other one."

Pete spat, then grunted as he said, "That right? Well come on over here, liveryman."

The man hesitated. Pete dropped his hand down onto the butt of the Schofield. The man did as he was told.

"Now, mister. I want ya to do a walk-around on that there mule."

Again, the man hesitated. Pete cocked the hammer on the Schofield.

"Ya can either walk around him, or get blowed through him—your choice, mister."

The liveryman walked down the left side of the mule, then back to the front.

"I said around the mule, mister," growled Pete.

The owner was sweating now. Nervously, he eased his way around to the right side of the mule and moved slowly alongside the animal. As he neared the rear end, one of the mule's ears came up and the other dropped back. Pete saw it, but the others hadn't noticed the move. Pete kept his eyes on the liveryman as he hesitated, not wanting to walk behind the mule. He looked at Pete and saw he still had his hand on the butt of the .45. Seeing he had little choice, the liveryman tried to slip past the mule's rear end, but he was too slow. The mule's head dropped down and his hind legs kicked back with lightning speed, knocking the liveryman off his feet and into the clapboard fence. He lay there screaming in pain as he clutched his right leg with both hands and cried out, "The son of a bitch done broke my goddamn leg. Get a doctor—somebody go get the doctor, for God sakes!"

Matt and the others weren't sure what to say or to do. They were speechless. Taking the money from Matt's hands, Pete counted out forty dollars and gave the rest back to him. Moving over to the fence where the injured man sat crying in pain, Pete tossed the money at his feet.

"There's forty dollars—that's twenty a mule—all a cheatin' man deserves. Yer damn lucky to be gettin' paid at all after what ya tried. Now don't ya bother gettin' up. We'll find us a couple of mules on our own. Let's go, boys."

Pete found two other mules in the group and led them to the stable. Searching through the pile of harness and gear piled inside the door, he pulled out the rigging for the pack mules. He tossed it over to the boys, who just looked at it, not one of them having any idea what to do with it.

Pete shook his head. "Now I reckon yer gonna tell me ain't none of ya ever rigged a lop-ear for packin'—that right?"

Grabbing the harness up, he set to work rigging one of the mules.

"Ya boys better watch this close. I ain't gonna be doin' it again."

The three men gathered around to watch what Pete was doing. In the background, the liveryman was screaming again for a doctor. No one paid any attention to him.

"How'd ya know that mule was gonna kick that fella, Pete?" asked Matt.

Pete kept working as he answered. "The mule was blind in his right eye. Causes him to get jittery when anybody starts round on his blind side, 'specially when that person got around his ass end."

"So that's what all that steppin' back an' forth was all about," said Billy.

"That's right, boy. When I moved, saw only one eye followin' me back and forth."

Pete finished his work and stepped back. "Okay, boys,

this one's ready. That other one is yers. Hope ya was payin' attention."

When J.T. and Abe pulled up to the livery with a wagon load of supplies, they found Pete trying his best not to laugh as he watched the three men arguing among themselves about which way the slip harness was supposed to go. Like the others, J.T. was surprised by Pete's clean, neat appearance. The two men stepped down from the wagon.

"Abe, meet Shotgun Pete Simmons. Pete, this is Abe Covington, uncle of the two kids we're goin' after."

As Abe reached out to shake hands with Pete, he said, "I've heard of you."

"Same here, Cap'n."

"What'd we got goin' on over there?" asked J.T.

Pete laughed. "Them boys 'pose to be riggin' that mule for carryin', but 'pears more like they gettin' him ready to put on the spit, don't it?"

All three men laughed before Pete said, "Reckon I better help out or we'll never get outta here."

For the first time J.T. noticed the man inside the corral, sitting on the ground and leaning against the fence. He was obviously in pain and holding his leg with both hands. The livery owner couldn't scream anymore, his voice was gone.

"What's the story on that fella at the fence there, Pete?" asked J.T.

"That's the livery owner," said Pete as he pushed the boys back and began taking the upside-down rigging off the mule. "He tried to stiff the boys here with a couple of ringers. Damn mule kicked hell out of him—broke his leg."

"Shouldn'd we get him some help?" asked Abe.

"Hell, no!" grumbled Pete. "He was willin' to let that poor critter with a bad leg carry a load to Mexico—he can damn well get his self over to the doc. See how he likes walkin' on a bad leg, by God."

Abe grinned over at J.T. Pete Simmons was going to fit in just fine.

It was just past noon when the six men and two pack mules headed out of Laredo. They had only been on the trail for a couple of hours before J.T. noticed a large group of birds circling in the sky off to the north. He pointed them out to Abe. At the same time Pete rode up.

"Ya'll seen 'em too, did ya?"

"Buzzards?" asked Abe.

Pete spat, then answered. "Yeah, I'd say so. Maybe even a flock of crows as well. Somethin' dead over that way, I reckon. Whatever it is must be pretty big to draw that many."

"What's over that way, Pete?"

"Nothin', 'ceptin' the Casa Blanco Pass."

J.T. looked over at Abe. "You wanta take a ride over an' have a look?"

Abe thought about it for a moment, then replied, "Nope. We got problems of our own. Them kids is all that's on my mind right now. We got no time to go lookin' for more trouble."

No more was said about the matter. An hour later, the men and their mules were crossing the Rio Grande into Mexico.

SEVEN

✶

WHILE FRANK AND Mitch were drinking at the cantina in San Pedro, Chacon had been busy finding a wagon big enough to carry their prize. After an hour of searching, he finally found what he was looking for. Paying the owner twice what it was worth, he sent it back with the three *vaqueros,* telling them to help transfer the ammo and head for the Den. He and the two gringos would catch up later.

A mile south of San Pedro, John T. Law and his outfit stopped and set up camp for the night. After gathering up firewood and having a meal of beans and taters, J.T. chose Harvey and Billy to stay and guard the camp while he and the others rode into San Pedro to see if they could get a lead on the Comancheros. They were going to need information if they were going to have any chance at all of finding this band of renegades. Right now all they knew for sure was that the Comancheros had a hideout somewhere in the mountains. But the Sierras were a vast mountain range that stretched out for miles. They could search for years and never find the place they were looking for. They were going to have to ask questions, but do it in such a way so as not to draw suspicion. There was little doubt that the Comancheros had eyes and ears working for them in nearly every village and town between the Rio and their mountain fortress. It wouldn't take them long to hear that a group of gringos were asking questions.

Abe and J.T. had thought of that before they left Austin. The only Americans running around down in that part of the woods were either prospectors or men on the run. They were going to need a story, something to justify their being there. It was the wanted poster on the McMasters boys that gave Abe the idea. He sent a wire to a printer friend of his in Laredo. He asked him to make up a stack of wanted posters. The flyers were to include the detailed descriptions of himself, J.T., Billy, and the McMasters boys. Of course, Pete wasn't on them, but that wouldn't be a problem. Pete already had at least four different ones out on him already. The printer was to put a one-thousand-dollar reward on the top and list the gang's crimes as murder and bank robbery. They were wanted dead or alive.

The posters were ready and waiting the morning they left Laredo. As soon as they had crossed the Rio, they had started placing the posters on trees, fences, and anywhere else they would be easily visible. If anyone should happen to ask, they would deny they were the men on the posters, but if pressed hard enough, they planned to give in and admit that they were the bank robbers, and that they were hiding out in Mexico until things died down a bit. The main thing was to convince people that they were outlaws—ruthless and dangerous men who were capable of anything.

It was dusk when the four men rode into the town. There were three cantinas along the street.

"Where you wanta start?" ask Abe.

"This first one's as good as any," said J.T.

Tying their horses off in front of the cantina, J.T. gathered the men around him.

"Okay now, boys. Remember. We'll do some drinkin', but I don't want anybody gettin' drunk. We just want people to think we are. We'll toss some money around, then after a while, we'll start gettin' loud and rowdy to draw some attention—that part shouldn't be too hard. Keep an eye out for anyone that might show a special interest in us. That'll be the fellow on the Comancheros' payroll, or at least one of 'em. We ready?"

Abe and Matt nodded. Pete tipped his hat back as he said, "Let's go. Hell, I'm thirsty."

Drawing attention to themselves wasn't going to be a problem—not with Pete Simmons along. As they entered the cantina, Pete let out an ear-splitting rebel yell and shouted, "Hang onto yer women, ya sons a bitches—Shotgun Pete Simmons and the boys are in town!"

Pete slurred his words and staggered around just enough to convince everyone in the place that he was well on his way to an all-night drunk. Surprised by Pete's sudden outburst, J.T. and the others quickly joined in.

"Drinks on the house, amigos!" shouted Abe, tossing a stack of money onto the bar.

"Yahoo!" cried Matt as he reached down and slapped

the ass of one of the barmaids carrying a tray full of drinks.

J.T. gave a yell, then reached over and pulled a young woman from the lap of a *vaquero*. He began dancing her around and around, his boots kicking up dust from the dirt floor, bringing a howl of protest from nearby tables.

The owner, a short, potbellied little man with a long mustache, hurried from behind the bar.

"Please—please, *señor*. We do not dance in here. Too much dust. Come—come, I will show you to a table. Maria! A bottle of our finest whiskey and four glasses. *Rápido!*"

The little man led the group to a table toward the back of the cantina, hoping to distance them from the other patrons, who were still upset over their unruly entrance. An attractive young girl with dark eyes and coat-black, waist-length hair appeared at their table with the whiskey and glasses. She looked to be no more than fifteen or sixteen years old. Matt started to reach out and grab her, but a disapproving look from J.T. quickly brought Matt's hand back to the table.

"*Gracias, señorita. Cuánto?*" asked J.T.

"*Dos dólares, señor.*"

J.T. gave her two dollars, then pressed a five-dollar gold piece in her hand, then pointed to her. "For you. *Comprendes?*"

Her eyes lit up when she saw how much money he had given her. With a big smile and a slight giggle, she replied, "*Sí señor, muchas gracias.*" Then she hurried back to her work.

Relative calm had returned to the cantina as Pete began pouring drinks for everyone. J.T. leaned over the table and in a low tone said, "Jesus, Pete. You sure know how to get a crowd's attention. What was that all about anyway?"

Pete grinned. "Hell, son, why drag it out? Might as well get their damn attention early. Let 'em know we're here and we're on the prowl. In my prime I used to walk into places like this with my scattergun an' blow a hole in the roof—now that'll get folks' attention. Hell, that little yellin' there weren't nothin'."

They all laughed and downed their drinks. In a corner, a man with a guitar began to play a festive tune. The hunt for Debbie and Thomas had begun in earnest. There would be no turning back.

AS THE NIGHT progressed, they continued their rowdy ways, all the time watching the room for anyone suspicious. But other than the usual go-to-hell looks that most gringos got from the locals, no one was really paying much attention to them. Pete shouted to the owner for another bottle. When the girl brought it to the table, J.T. smiled at her and asked, "Have any other gringos been here today, *señorita*?"

She grinned at him. She had the whitest teeth he had ever seen.

"*Sí*. We get many here sometimes. *Dos norte americanos* were here not long ago. But they left maybe hours ago."

"You know where they went?"

"No say, *señor*. Another cantina maybe. I must go."

"Thank you."

"*De nada!*"

Abe glanced across the table at John Law. "What'd you think, John?"

"I think it's time we moved on down the street."

The four men walked out into the street. It was a crisp clear night. The sky was filled with stars. Matt inhaled deeply, then let it out. "A fellow don't know how sweet fresh night air is till he's spent some time in one of them places."

Untying their horses, the four men walked them down the street a short distance until they came to another cantina.

"Okay, Pete. No hell-raisin' this time. We just go in, get us a table, an' see what happens. You got that?" said J.T.

Pete shook his head. "Okay, we'll do it yer way this time."

When they walked inside, they paused at the door and looked around the room. If they hadn't walked their horses up the street, they'd swear they had walked right back into the same place they had just left. There weren't as many people and the smoke and dust weren't as bad, but that was about the only difference. They found a table and called for a bottle. J.T. looked around the room for any signs of other Americans. There were none.

A large, heavyset woman with huge breasts brought them a bottle and some glasses. She spoke English.

"Three dollars, *señor*."

Abe placed three dollars in her hand, then held up two more.

"*Señora,* have you seen any other gringos here tonight?"

The big woman eyed the money, then nodded her head. "*Sí, señor*. Three men left only a little while ago. Two were gringos."

"Are they staying in San Pedro?"

She shrugged her shoulders. "No sé. I only see them tonight for the first time. But there is another one who has been here for a week now. He was here this morning, but I no see him tonight."

Abe gave her the money, which she quickly pushed down between her bulging breasts. *"Gracias, señora,"* he said.

Pouring a drink, Abe slumped back in his chair. "Looks another dry hole, John."

J.T. sat with his back to the wall watching the front door. "It's early yet, Abe." One hour passed into two, then three. People came and went from the cantina without giving the Americans more than a glance. Abe had had enough.

"I say we call it a night, J.T., an' get on back to camp. We could all use some sleep."

John Law agreed. They were finishing their drinks and about to leave when four *vaqueros* came through the door. Halfway to the bar, one of them saw the Americans. As his friends made their way to the bar, he paused and stared at J.T. and the others. He pulled a folded piece of paper from his coat and studied it for a moment, then looked their way again. Keeping the paper in his hand, he quickly walked over to his three friends, placed the paper on the bar, and nodded back toward the gringos' table. As all four men stared at them, J.T. muttered, "Hold on, boys."

Pete and the others had been about to stand up when J.T. spoke. They all looked back to the bar and slowly sat back down. The paper was passed around among the *vaqueros* as Matt said, "That's one of our flyers."

"Sure enough." muttered Abe.

The men talked among themselves for a few minutes. Then one of them took the flyer and left while the other three moved to the end of the bar to keep an eye on J.T. and the others.

"How you figure this, J.T.?" asked Abe.

"We done sparked somebody's interest. I'm bettin' they sent that fella for some more help."

"Think these boys could be part of the bunch we're lookin' for?" asked Matt.

"Could be, Matt. But I don't think so. I figure these fellows are lookin' to collect the reward money we put on that poster."

Pete laughed. "Now there's a switch. Some folks lookin' to collect a bounty on a bounty man, an' the damn poster ain't even on the up-an' up."

J.T. was about to tell Pete to shut up when the fourth man reappeared. He stood in the doorway and signaled for his three friends to join him outside.

"Pete, you got your shotgun with you?" asked J.T.

"Hell, yes. Got her on a leather thong hangin' inside this here new coat ya bought me."

"You expectin' trouble?" asked Matt.

"I don't figure that fella called them boys outside to talk about the weather."

"How many you figure?" asked Abe.

"Those four, an' however many he went after when he left here. Ain't no tellin'."

Abe looked around the cantina. "Don't see no back door, an' there ain't no damn windows. How you wanta work this?"

"Ain't but one way, Abe. We go out that door and hope we get clear of it before they start throwin' lead," said J.T.

John Law and the men stood up. Pulling their guns, they checked to make sure they had full loads. They kept the weapons in their hands. Pete swung the shotgun out from under his coat. The people in the cantina began moving from the bar and tables, heading to the back of the room, wanting to get as far away from the door as possible. Not one even considered leaving out the front.

The men moved to the door, standing to the side. The silence was broken by the sound of hammers going back.

J.T. looked at each man. "Once we're outside, spread out. If a man goes down, we stay with him. Agreed?"

They all nodded their approval. "Okay—let's go!"

J.T. was the first one out. Once clear of the door, he went to the right. Abe came out next and followed J.T. Pete and Matt were next and broke to the left. They expected to be greeted by a hail of gunfire, but instead found themselves staring at an empty street. No people and no horses except for their own, which were still tied exactly where they had left them. Their eyes searched the alleyways and the rooftops, the doorways and storefronts, but there was nothing—not a single person.

"What the hell's goin' on, boys?" asked Matt.

Even the old wily veteran was at a loss.

"Strange. Yes, sir, mighty strange," said Pete.

J.T. had expected to find their horses gone. That was what he would have done. But since the *vaqueros* had been so kind as to leave them, it was time to put them to use, and fast.

"Matt, you and Pete get mounted. We'll keep you covered."

Pete quickly unhooked the scattergun from the leather thong; then he and Matt swung up into their saddles. They turned their horses out toward the street as Pete yelled back, "Okay boys, swing up, we got the street."

J.T. and Abe mounted, then moved out front with J.T.

taking the lead. Glancing back over his shoulder, he said, "Nice and easy, boys. We ain't out of here yet."

Their guns still out, cocked and ready, the four men began walking their horses toward the north road leading out of town. For a minute, it looked as if they might make it without any trouble, but that was not the case.

Four riders suddenly appeared from behind a building at the end of the street. They were quickly joined by four more that came out of an alleyway. They swung their horses in a line blocking the way out of town. Abe, Matt, and Pete spread out behind John Law.

"Two to one," whispered Abe.

"Hell, any less'd take the fun out of it, Abe," said Pete with a laugh as he slid a finger over both triggers of the shotgun and whispered, "Ya make the call, Boss."

"Hold off with that cannon, Pete, till we see what they got to say," cautioned J.T.

J.T. closed to within thirty feet of the line, then stopped. Leaning forward, he crossed his arms over his saddlehorn, the .45 clearly visible, asking, "There somethin' we can do for you boys?"

J.T. studied the men before him as he waited for an answer. They were all Mexicans. Three held rifles laid across their saddles. The others all carried pistols, their hands resting on the grips, ready for whatever was going to happen next.

A big man with a broad-brimmed sombrero moved his horse forward a few steps. His dark tanned face and black deep-set eyes sized up J.T. and the men behind him.

"Where you come from, gringo? Why you in my town?"

J.T. gave the man a friendly smile. "No place in particular. Just passing through. Figured we'd have a few drinks 'fore movin' on. Didn't know this was your town."

The big Mexican laughed. "Oh, *señor,* I think maybe you not tell Poco the truth. My friend, he have a paper that say you and your amigos, maybe you rob a bank in Texas, maybe even kill a few people, no?"

"Well, your friend's mistaken. We don't know anything about that. Like I said, we're just passin' through."

Poco grinned, showing brownish-yellow tobacco-stained teeth.

"Passing through my town can be very expensive, *señor.*"

"Is that right?"

"*Sí.* We have a tax to visit our lovely town. It is a special tax for gringos who . . . how you say . . . are passin' through. But for men such as you that are in the banking business, what is a few hundred dollars? So you pay your tax like good gringos and you and your amigos can go with God. What you say, huh?"

J.T. grinned as he sat up straight in the saddle, his hand holding the .45 resting on the saddlehorn.

"Poco, we don't want no trouble. But if you don't move your men out of our way, you're gonna find out just how expensive that damn tax of yours can be."

The Mexican leader's grin faded. He straightened himself in the saddle. There was a look of fury in his face as he barked, *"Hijo de puta!"*

"Uh-oh," said Abe. "You went an' made him mad, J.T. I think he just called you a son of a bitch."

"I know. Get ready."

Poco shifted in his saddle as he glanced back at his men. When he turned back toward J.T., he was already pulling his pistol. In the blink of an eye, the street erupted in a thundering roar of gunfire, screams of pain, and the cries of dying men.

J.T. and Abe both fired at the same time, both bullets hitting Poco in chest. The big man jerked backward, then fell dead from his horse. The deafening roar of Pete's shotgun blew two men in the line out of their saddles. Matt fired twice, taking another one down with a shot to the chest and the head. As he started to fire again, he felt his shirt pull and a burning in his right arm as a bullet tore a hole through his shirt. J.T. snapped off two more shots at a man arising his rifle. Both shots were on the mark. The man crumpled over and fell to the ground.

Pete's Schofield went into action, knocking a man off his horse. As the man started to get up, Pete put a shot through his head. In a panic, the remaining two Mexicans pulled rein and tried to cut and run, but it was too late. They were caught up in a hailstorm of lead that sent both men tumbling from their horses. Their bodies hit the ground, rolled once, then came to rest among the bodies of their friends who lay dead in the narrow street.

In a little less than a minute, eight men had died. Gunsmoke hung over the street like a swamp fog. The smell of cordite was heavy in the night air. People in the town slowly began to peek out the doors and windows as Pete leaned over and checked Matt's arm.

The bullet had cut a clean groove through the skin and muscle, leaving a gaping open wound that made it look worse than it really was.

"Yer all right, boy," said Pete in his usual gruff tone. "We get back to camp, I'll sew that up for ya."

J.T. saw Abe leaning to the side in the saddle.

"Abe, you hit?"

"Don't know—can't feel my damn leg."

J.T. started to swing down to check, but Abe told him to stay in the saddle. He could still ride. They could have a look at it in camp. Right now, it was a good idea to get clear of San Pedro before any of Poco's friends showed up. Walking their horses through the body-littered street, the four men rode out of town. They had been in Mexico less than twenty-four hours and eight men were already dead. There were going to be a lot more before this thing was over.

As the sounds of the four horsemen faded into the night, a man stepped from the alleyway and walked among the dead sprawled in the street. Pausing at the body of Poco, the notorious bandit and killer, the man reached down and removed a piece of paper sticking out of the dead man's pocket. As more people began to gather at the scene, the man moved into the light of the cantina. Unfolding the paper, he took his time reading it. When he had finished, he folded it again and placed it inside his coat pocket. Walking away, he muttered to himself, "Two thousand dollars reward is not enough for men that can fight like that."

EIGHT

✴

BILL PURVIS WAS in a bad mood when he led the Army wagons through the gates of the Devil's Den. The news he found waiting for him didn't make him feel any better. Tired and worried, he hadn't made it as far as the house before Mamacita Vescuz came running across the compound. As she looked up at him and clutched his leg, Purvis saw a glint of fear in her eyes. Her voice trembling, she quickly told him that two of the men had tried to rape the young gringo girl. Purvis's eyes went red with fury. Swinging his big frame out of the saddle, he grabbed the woman by both arms and began to shake her.

"How the hell did that happen? Where were you?"

He slapped her hard across the face, the blow sending her reeling to the ground.

"Goddamnit, woman, you were supposed to be watchin' out for her. Where is she?"

Cowering on the ground, the woman sobbed, *"La casa! La casa!"*

The rage in him building, Purvis stepped over the woman and hurried up to the house. As he walked in, he found Hector Valdez, one of his most trusted lieutenants, standing over the little girl, watching as two young women tended to the cuts and scratches that covered her body.

Moving to the couch, Purvis knelt down next to her. What he saw made him angry and sad at the same time. Her young face was battered and bruised. There was an open gash on her lower lip and scratches on her young breasts. It was clear that the young girl had put up a fight. Looking to one of the women, he asked, "Did they rape her?"

The woman shook her head. *"Nada."*

Purvis stood up. His hellish gaze fell upon Valdez.

"Where are the men that did this?"

"I had them taken to the whipping post. I figured you'd want to deal with this yourself."

"Ya goddamn right I do. Come on!"

Valdez was right behind Purvis as the big man stomped out of the house and across the compound toward the corral. The wagon drivers were just stepping down from their rigs when they saw Purvis coming their way, followed by a crowd of people.

"Wonder what the hell that's all about," said one of the men in the crowd.

"Don't know. But from the look on the boss's face, I'm glad I ain't got nothin' to do with it," said another.

As the crowd passed the wagons, a driver asked. "What's going on?"

"Gonna be a killin'," was the reply.

The crowd spread out behind Purvis, not wanting to get too close to the leader when he was in one of his moods. They never knew for certain what he might do. More than once, Purvis had lost his temper and struck out at the nearest person around him to vent his anger.

The two accused men had been stripped to the waist and chained to a thick seven-foot pole known as the whipping post. It was used to administer punishment for crimes committed within the compound, like stealing, knife-fighting, and drunken shootings.

As soon as Purvis walked up to the post, one of the men began pleading for mercy. The other man didn't bother. It was plain by the look on his face and the emptiness in his eyes that he had resigned himself to his fate. As Purvis stepped up to the post, a silence fell over the crowd.

"Please, Señor Bill. I wanted no part in what happened. I was drunk on tequila. I didn't know what I was doing." Nodding at the other man, he went on. "It was him. He filled my head with bad thoughts. He made me help him."

Purvis ignored the pleading man. Looking at the other one, he asked, "That true? You were drunk an' didn't know what the hell ya was doin'?"

The expression on the man's face never changed as he calmly replied. "Hell, no, that's not true. We drank a little bit, then started talkin' about the young gringo bitch. She is young and a virgin. The more we talked, the more we wanted her, so we went down there to fuck her. That's the truth."

"He lies, Señor Bill!" screamed the other man. "Please,

Señor Bill, don't listen to his lies." Looking into the other man's eyes, the coward shouted, *"Bastardo!* I will . . ."

Before the man could finish, Purvis drew his Colt. 45 and blew the top of the man's head off. As the echoing sound of the shot faded among the mountains, Purvis holstered his gun and told Valdez to give the other man ten lashes and release him. The truth had saved his life. The crowd parted as Purvis walked up to the house. As far as they were concerned, their leader's action had been swift and just. One had begged and lied like the coward he was, while the other had shown courage and admitted to his wrongdoing, and was willing to accept the consequences for his actions. Bill Purvis respected that in a man.

Valdez followed Purvis up to the house. He could tell there was more troubling the Comanchero leader than the attempted rape of the young captive. As they entered the house, the women asked what they should do with the girl. Did he want her placed back in the cage? Bill wasn't taking any more chances. He told them to get the boy and bring him to the house. The children would stay in his room until the exchange. He would sleep elsewhere. The women were to stay with them and not let them out of their sight. If anything else should happen, they would face the same fate as the man at the whipping post.

Having settled the situation with the children, a tired and troubled Bill Purvis slumped down in a chair at his desk. Valdez went the bar and poured them each a tall glass of whiskey. Setting one in front of his boss, he walked around and set down in a chair in front of the desk.

"I didn't see Chacon or Lee and Taggart with you."

Purvis took a long slow pull on the whiskey.

"Damn wagon spoked out on us. They went to find another one. They'll be along soon."

"Looks like everything went pretty well with the raid. You got what you went after."

Purvis set his glass down on the desk and frowned. "It went to shit, that's where it went. We lost nine damn good men and four shot all to hell. Thirteen men, Valdez—thirteen! That's thirteen guns we won't have with us when we go to meet with that damn renegade Notonte."

Valdez now understood the worried looked he had noticed earlier. The meeting with Notonte was in four days. They had dealt with the Apache warrior before, but Valdez had never trusted the man. On more than one occasion he had sensed that if it were not for the fact that Purvis had brought all of the well-armed Comancheros to the meetings, the war chief would have simply killed them and taken what he wanted. If he would consider that over a few wagon loads of flour, blankets, and whiskey, it was a damn good bet he'd risk it all for two hundred rifles and two wagon loads of ammunition. Purvis had asked twenty thousand dollars in gold for the rifles and the bullets. Notonte and his warriors had had a month to collect the gold. The problem was, they wouldn't know if Notonte had it or not until they arrived at the rendezvous site.

Looking at his boss, Valdez asked, "If Notonte don't have the gold, what'd you think he'll do?"

Purvis stared at his whiskey glass as he slowly turned it in his hands. That was a good question. If Notonte had the gold, he saw no problem. He was even going to throw in the two kids as a show of good faith. But if he didn't have the gold, things could go bad in a hurry. At last count, the war chief had close to fifty warriors. With two hundred rifles, he could recruit another hundred with little or no effort. That many Apache, armed with new Winchester repeating rifles, would place Notonte in command of a force capable of defeating any army in Mexico. Gold or no gold, Notonte had to have those rifles, no matter what the cost.

Looking over at Valdez, he answered the man's question.

"He'll try to kill every man-jack of us. Count on it."

Valdez took a drink, then calmly said, "We're going to need some more men."

"I know. But we only got four days. Where we gonna find 'em?"

Valdez thought about it for a moment, then said, "For enough gold maybe Poco and his men will go along. I'll send a couple of men to San Pedro to see if he'll join us."

OUTSIDE, CHACON AND the others had caught up to the wagon just as it was about to enter the compound. As they rode by the corral, Lee pointed to the man chained at the post with the top of his head gone.

"Now, I'll bet there's a hell of a story to go along with that."

"Yeah," said Chacon. "Looks like some of Bill's work."

The wagon headed for the barn while the men went to the corral. Taggart was taking the saddle off his horse when he noticed Dog coming through the gates. When the half-breed saw the man at the post, he leaped from his horse with his knife in his hand. The gunfighter turned away as Dog began to saw at the dead man's ear.

NINE

✦

MATT LET OUT a howl as Pete poked the sewing needle in for a final time and ran the horsehair stitch across and out the other side. He pulled it tight and tied it off, then slapped Matt on his bare back.

"There ya' go, sonny. Good as new. Be a little sore for a few days, but ya won't be getting' the gan-green neither."

Matt reached for his shirt. "Thanks, Pete."

Harvey grabbed his brother's shirt and held it for him while Matt slipped it on. Harvey had been in a near panic when they rode into camp and he saw that his brother had been bloodied in a fight. He had fussed over his older brother like a mother hen. Matt had tried to act tough about it, telling Harvey to leave him alone, that it was nothing but a scratch. But it was obvious to the others that there was a great deal of love between the two brothers.

The feeling had began to return to Abe's leg by the time they reached camp. Closer examination found that he hadn't been hit, but his boot had taken the shot. The bullet had cut a line just under the stirrup and taken the heel of his boot off. The impact had numbed the nerves in the leg, causing a loss of feeling from the knee down.

Later that night, as they sat around the campfire, J.T. filled Billy and Harvey in on what had happened in San Pedro. Both young men expressed their disappointment at not having been there. Abe told them not to worry, there was going to be plenty of shooting before this was over.

"What's our next move?" asked Billy.

"I think it would be a good idea to get out of here by first light," said J.T. "Just in case some of Poco's friends decide to come looking for us."

"I say we head west for Candela. It's a fair-size town. Might be the comancheros get their supplies out of there," said Abe.

"Sounds good to me," said J.T. "My idea damn near got us killed."

"Awh, hell, boy, that weren't yer fault," said Pete as he spat a stream of tobacco juice to the ground. "These here mountains are full of bandits. No tellin' when ya goin' run into the bastards. But they all got one thing in common—they hate gringos."

"We gonna keep a man on watch?" asked Matt.

"Won't hurt. Harvey, you go first. Two hours on, then wake the next man. The rest of us better get some sleep. Gonna be a long day tomorrow," said Abe.

•   •   •

AT MIDDAY, THE rescuers rode into one of the countless villages that couldn't be found on any map and had a name known only to the locals in the region. It seemed as good a place as any to stop and rest the horses and the men as well. There was no café or cantina, but as soon as the men retired to the shade of some trees, women began to appear from their homes with bowls of beans and tortillas to sell for a modest price. The men gladly paid for their dinner. Soon, an old man came over to them with a jug and offered it to them for a dollar. It was homemade whiskey made from cactus juice. It had a bite like a snake and a kick like a horse.

After a full meal and a few drinks, Pete asked, "Cap'n, did you talk to the Yankee soldiers at the fort in Laredo 'bout maybe gettin' some help?"

"Yeah, I did, Pete. Colonel in charge wasn't there. Talk to his second in command, Major Pickett. He said they couldn't do anything for me as long as they had the kids across the Rio. Gave me a speech about borders and treaties an' all that political horseshit. Said it'd take somethin' mighty serious to get the Army to cross over. Matter of fact, he did his best to discourage me crossin' the border on my own. Said they couldn't do nothin' for us if we got caught."

"Yep, I was afraid of that. Would've been comfortin' knowin' them soldier boys was waitin' at the Rio. I got a feelin' we'll be runnin' hard with a pack of them Comancheros right on our ass once we got hold of them kids."

"You wantin' out, Pete?" asked Harvey.

"Didn't say such now, did I, ya pup? Why, I recall the time . . ."

With that, Pete went into another one of his stories from the old days. Although the tales were often wild, no doubt they were true, just exaggerated a little at times. Pete and the others were all so busy enjoying themselves, no one noticed the four men that rode in from the other end of the village. They had been hidden by the adobe houses.

The four men reined in behind one of the homes and dismounted. Quietly, their guns drawn, they worked their way around behind their prey, using the thick mesquite and small oak to cover their approach. J.T. and Pete were the first to sense their presence. Pete grabbed for his shotgun. J.T. started to draw his Peacemaker.

"Hold! You got no chance. Throw them hands high and do it now!" shouted a voice from the trees.

"Damnit all to hell. They caught us flat-footed, boys," said Abe. "Do what they say. They got us covered all the way around."

Abe and the others rose to their feet, their hands held high over their heads. The four emerged from the trees, their guns leveled on the group. As they stepped closer, J.T. stared at the tall man in the black hat with the silver hatband.

"Dave? Is that you?"

The tall man stepped closer. "J.T.? J.T. Law? Well, I'll be damned. John Thomas, what the hell are you doin' in Mexico?"

J.T. started to lower his hands. One of the Mexican gunmen cocked back the hammer on his .45.

"Hold it, Juan. You boys put your guns away. This fella's a friend of mine."

Pete and the others let out a sigh of relief as J.T. said, "Hell, Dave, I could ask you the same thing."

"Well, we thought we were gonna be two thousand dollars richer before the day was out. My boy Juan there was downright positive that you fellows were the men on this here poster we found yesterday. Gotta admit, these descriptions are a pretty good fit to you boys."

"Ought to. We had 'em made up special for just that reason."

Dave shook his head. "Dead good way to get yourself killed. Guess you know that. You wanta tell me why a bounty man would wanta be on a poster? An' who are all these other fellows? Guess they ain't wanted for nothin' either, right?"

J.T. laughed. "Well, yes an' no. This tall fellow here with the mustache is Abe Covington. He's a captain in the Texas Rangers."

J.T. though Dave was going to swallow his chew of tobacco when he heard that.

"The young fellow next to him is Billy Tyler, another Ranger," said J.T. "Them two boys there are the Mc-Masters brothers, Matt and Harvey. An' the elder of the group, that's Shotgun Pete Simmons. Quite a crew, don't you think?"

"Hell, I reckon," said Dave. "Now you really got me curious. I seen a poster on the brothers couple months ago up in Kansas. As for Pete, hell, I thought he was dead. An' two Texas Rangers roamin' around in Mexico—they either got a death wish or you boys got something damn important goin' on down here. You wanta let me in on it?"

J.T. reached out and put his hand on Dave's shoulder as he made the introduction. "Gentlemen, I'd like you all to meet Dave Matther. Dave's been a lawman, bounty hunter, and some say an outlaw, but that's never been proved. He's a hell of a man with a gun in a scrap. Trust me on that. I've seen him in action. Pull up a rock an' seat yourself, Dave, an' I'll tell you why we're down here. Maybe you can help us out."

When J.T. had finished his story, he said, "That's about it, Dave. We're determined to get them kids back come hell or high water. Problem is, we got no idea where the comancheros might be holed up."

Dave turned to the man named Juan and rattled off some rapid-fire Spanish. The man nodded his head and replied in kind. It was so fast that J.T. only caught part of it. Something about hidden arroyos and the devil?

"Sorry, J.T. I forgot. This here is Juan Romero. I've been keeping company with his sister. These other two boys are his cousins. They've all had run-ins with the Comancheros. They raided Juan's village about two months ago. Killed three men and a woman. Took four women and three kids with 'em when they rode out. Juan and the cousins went after 'em, but lost the trail after sundown near the Chomais Pass."

"How far is that from here?" asked Abe.

"Oh, maybe twenty, thirty miles north of here."

Abe's eyes lit up. There was anxiety in his voice as he said, "What are we waitin' for? Let's get in the saddle."

"I know you're worried 'bout them kids, Captain, an' I don't blame you. But you don't wanta go runnin' hell-bent for leather into the Chomais. That's Notonte terri-tory," said Dave.

"Damn!" said Pete. "That murderin' Apache still runnin' loose? He's one mean hombre."

"Apaches!" shouted Matt. "Ya didn't say nothin' about Apaches, John Law. Comancheros, that's one thing, but Apaches, goddamn."

"Pete's right," said Dave. "He's a mean son of a bitch.

Skinned a couple of farmers a few days ago and roasted the poor bastards over a fire."

"He been raidin' a lot around these parts?" asked J.T.

"That's the funny part. He used to hit a place or two every month or so, grab up some women and supplies, stuff like that, but here lately, he's been damn busy. Hit over ten towns and villages in the last three weeks, ain't took nothin' but money and gold. Got a force of maybe sixty—seventy warriors ridin' with him, an' more showin' up every day. I don't know what it is, but he's up to somethin'. Normally, Apaches don't care about gold or money."

"That is strange," said J.T. "Unless . . ."

"Unless what, J.T.? What're you thinkin'?" asked Dave.

"If they're needin' gold, then I'd say the Comancheros must have something those Apaches want awful bad."

Abe's first thought was of the kids.

"No, it's more than just the kids, Abe. Usually, they try to barter these deals. This one is for gold and cash only. But what is it?"

"Hell, we ain't gonna find out settin' here," growled Pete.

"Dave, you and the boys wanta come along?" asked J.T. "Won't lie to you—we could use the help findin' that Chomais Pass."

Dave looked over at Juan, who nodded that he was willing to go along. The two cousins, however, had no desire to go hunting trouble with an army of Comancheros, and especially not with Notonte and his Apaches. The cousins rode off to the south to tell Juan's sister her brother and her lover would not be coming home for a while. The army of rescuers, now numbering eight, turned their horses north and began their journey toward the Chomais Pass.

Along the way, Matther told J.T. all he knew about the Comancheros. From what he had heard, the group was led by an American, a fella calling himself Big Bill Purvis. His second in command was a Mexican named Pablo Chacon, the son of a notorious Mexican bandit who had been the leader of the famed Comanchero band that had wreaked havoc on the residents of west Texas in the early seventies. The bandit leader had met his fate at the hands of Colonel Randle Mackenzie's U.S. cavalry in the last big battle of the Red River War. His son was now following in his father's footsteps. There were also stories that there were two gringo gunmen that rode with Purvis. Matther had not heard any names, but they were said to be men of exceptional talent with a gun.

As the sun began to set and the sky took on a purple haze, they came across a small stream that ran down from the mountains. It seemed a good place to spend the night. There was fresh water for the horses, and the terrain provided an excellent defense in case of attack. Abe protested at first. He wanted to continue on into the night. Every minute they delayed was another minute Debbie and Thomas had to endure God knows what from their captors. The others could understand the Ranger's torment, but both Dave and Juan told him that to wander about in the foothills and arroyos of the pass was akin to committing suicide. If the bandits, Comancheros, or Apaches did not kill you, the terrain itself could. Some of the arroyos had sheer drop-offs that could easily kill both a horse and rider. Reluctantly, Abe agreed to setting up camp for the night.

After a supper of beans, bacon, and fried taters, the

order of guard duty for the night was established. The horses had been hobbled, and one man would be awake at all times. Matt took the first watch, positioning himself on a small knoll surrounded by black brush and some small oaks. From there, he had a commanding view of the entire area around the campsite. One by one, the men began to head for their bedrolls and some much-needed sleep, until only Dave, J.T., and Abe remained around the small campfire.

"Ya seem to know quite abit about these Comancheros, Matther," said Abe. "No offense, but why is that?"

Matther pulled out the makings and began rolling himself a smoke.

"None taken, Captain. I been coming in and out of Mexico for years. Unlike a lot of Americans, I get along with these people pretty well. Learned to speak the language. Never looked down on 'em like I was better or somethin' just 'cause I was a gringo, always treated 'em as equals. That's about all any man asks for, Captain, just a little respect, no matter where they're from or what color they might be. As long as a man don't set himself up as better than others, hell, he can fit in anyplace. I just found my fit here in ol' Mexico, that's all."

"You say you been seein' Juan's sister. I'll bet she's a fine-looking woman, Dave," said J.T.

The two men could almost see the admiration in the man's eyes as he spoke.

"Oh, let me tell you, boys. Her name's Maria. She's a wonder. Got long black hair that shimmers when she walks and the most beautiful eyes I ever seen. An' when she talks, that low sultry voice of hers could stir the blood an' set a fella's heart to beatin' so fast, you think it's goin' to pop right out of your chest. Yes, sir. I'm damn lucky to have a woman like her."

"Don't you worry about her down here? I mean, with all these damn Comancheros and Apaches raidin' everything in sight. I mean, don't you worry about what could happen to her when you're gone? I'd think you'd want to take her out of here an' back to Texas," said Abe.

Dave exhaled a puff of smoke. His face took on a hard look as he gazed across at Abe. "Done that once. Caused a lot trouble. Took her to Laredo with me, figured she'd be safer there. Got us a room at a fine hotel. Took her out to supper that night. When we walked in, people looked at me as if I'd brought a dead cat into the place. Owner asked us to leave. He didn't want no 'Mexican whore' stinkin' up his place. I saw Maria's eyes well up with tears and she run outta the place. Well, guess I just lost it right then and there. 'Fore I knew it, I done knocked that fella over a table and was boot-stompin' him good until some other fella pulled me off him."

Dave paused a moment, dropped the stub of his smoke on the ground, and crushed it with his boot.

"I can't see where you done nothin' wrong," said Abe.

"Oh, that wasn't the trouble I was talkin' about, Captain. It was the two men I killed that caused all the trouble."

J.T. and Abe exchanged glances, then looked across at Dave as J.T. said, "Now I can see where that could change things just a mite. Who got killed?"

"Couple of cowboys. They grabbed Maria before she could get back to the hotel. Dragged her in an alley, tore her clothes, and was fixin' to mount her when I come out an' heard her scream. When I stepped into that alley, one of 'em had his pants down around his ankles and the other one was holdin' her down. I didn't say shit to 'em. Drew my gun and shot both the son of a bitches. Put three in each one of 'em. Was reloadin' to put in a few more when Maria grabbed me and pulled me outta there. We crossed back into Mexico that same night. Maria said she'd rather take her chances with the Apaches than go back across that river. Can't say I blame her much."

"They issue a warrant for you, Dave?" asked J.T.

"Hell, I reckon. I haven't crossed back over the Rio since that happened, so I don't know for sure. Don't much give a damn neither. Matter of fact, when I saw it was you we had treed today, I thought maybe they'd sent you across to bring me in."

J.T. shook his head. "That'll never happen, Dave. I don't hunt my friends."

"What time you figure we'll be at the pass tomorrow?" asked Abe.

"Sometime before noon, but I think it would benefit us to make a stop on the way."

"Where?" asked J.T.

"A friend of mine, Don Ricardo Sanchez, he has a hacienda a few miles this side of the pass. He knows everything that goes on in that area. He might have some information we could use."

"Lives a little close to the action, don't he?"

Dave laughed. "Sure does. But he keeps his own private army on the place. Got more guns than Fort Grant, an' a damn cannon to boot. The Comancheros hit him once and he hurt 'em bad. They ain't never tried again. Apaches got the same, but they're a stubborn bunch. They keep comin' back every now and then to have another go at it."

J.T. stretched his arms and legs. "That sounds like a

good idea, Dave. We'll stop by in the mornin'. I gotta get some sleep. Be my watch in a couple of hours."

As he stood up, J.T. looked down at Matther. "Dave, I want you to know I appreciate you and Juan comin' along with us. Thank you."

Matther looked up at the big man and nodded. "Glad we can help, John T."

Abe expressed his gratitude as well and went to bed, leaving Dave sitting alone. Tossing a stick into the fire, Matther looked around the campsite. What a strange mix of men he was riding with: Rangers, gunfighters, outlaws, and a bounty hunter. All with only one purpose: the rescue of a little girl and her brother. As strange as this group might seem, he was glad to be a part of it.

TEN

★

FRANK TAGGART SAT alone at a table in the corner of the bunkhouse. He had just finished cleaning his pistol, and was putting the final parts of the .45 back together, when Mitch Lee came through the door.

"Hey, Frank. Bill wants us up to the house pronto. Been some kind of trouble in San Pedro."

Taggart clinked the cylinder into place and spun it once. "I'll be along."

"He said now, Frank."

Taggart looked up at Lee. Frank's eyes were angry and there was a frown that worked its way across the gunfighter's face.

"You know, Lee, I'm gettin' damn tired of people barkin' orders at me like I was some kinda goddamn dog. Matter of fact, I'm tried of this fuckin' bunch. Stealing kids, cuttin' off ears, tryin' to rape a little girl—hell with that. I don't need this shit. Lord knows, I done some pretty bad things in my life, but ridin' with this outfit is about as low as a man can go. You can tell that big son of a bitch up there at the house that I quit."

Mitch Lee shook his head as he looked down at his friend.

"Frank, damnit, I told ya not to think about that shit. Three more days, we'll have more money than we ever saw before. We get that, hell, I leave with ya. Now come on. Ya know how he gets when he's kept waitin'. Let's go."

Taggart loaded the Colt. Standing, he strapped on his gunbelt and dropped the well-oiled pistol into place. "I meant what I said, Mitch. I'm through."

Turning away from his friend, Taggart began gathering his few belongings and stuffing them into his saddlebags.

"Big Bill ain't gonna like this, Frank. Not now. Not after losin' all them fellas at the ambush. I think he's really worried about this deal with Notonte. He's gonna want every gun he's got at that rendezvous in three days. He ain't likely to take you leavin' very well."

"Notonte's *his* problem, and I don't have to ask anybody about leavin'. I go where the hell I want, when I want. Ain't nobody gonna stop me either."

Lee knew by the look in his friend's eyes that any further talk was a waste of time. Stepping forward, he extended his hand.

"Still think yer makin' a mistake, partner. But if that's what ya wanta do, then good luck to ya. Maybe we'll cross trails again over in the States. Y' be careful, ya hear?"

Taggart slung his saddlebags over his broad shoulders.

Taking Lee's hand in a firm grip, he warned his friend, "You watch your back, Mitch."

Lee grinned. "Without ya around to mother-hen me, guess I'll have to. Now go on, get out of here. I'll stall for a while. Give ya a chance to get clear of here 'fore Bill knows yer gone. Adios, amigo."

Taggart took the back way around the bunkhouse to the corral. Quickly saddling his big bay, he swung up into the saddle. Looking back at the corner of the bunkhouse, he waved a final good-bye to Mitch Lee and rode away.

Chacon came out onto the front porch a few minutes later. Seeing Lee near the bunkhouse, he yelled to him, "Where's Taggart?" Lee looked back up toward the house, shrugged his shoulders, and shook his head from side to side.

"Well, forget it. Get on up here, now!" shouted Chacon.

Walking toward the house, Lee cast a glance back toward the pass. Silhouetted against the blue sky, he saw the final sentry placed at the pass entrance make a motion with his arm, a sign that Frank had made it past the final man who had any chance of stopping him from leaving the Devil's Den. Frank Taggart was on his way back to Texas.

Chacon yelled for Lee to hurry up and get in the house. He then shouted to Dog to find Taggart and bring the gunfighter to the house. The breed waved and set out to find the American.

Bill Purvis was in Lee's face the minute the gunman entered the room.

"Just where the hell ya been? An' where's Taggart?"

Again, Lee simply shrugged his shoulders. "Hell if I know. He wasn't in the bunkhouse or the kitchen. I got no idea where he is."

Chacon came into the room. "I sent Dog to look for him. He'll bring him here when he finds him. Now what is this about trouble in San Pedro?"

Purvis mumbled something about discipline, then said, "Poco's dead—him and seven of his best men."

Lee didn't say anything. But the look on Chacon's face was one of disbelief.

"That can't be true. Poco's got those people in that village scared to death of him. They wouldn't have the balls to try anything against him."

"Hell, it wasn't those piss-ant peons that killed 'em, ya idiot. It was gringos—four of 'em."

This sparked Lee's interest. Four Americans going up against Poco, who was a fair hand with a gun himself, and seven of his top guns. Two-to-one odds. That was interesting.

"Any of the Americans killed in the shootout?" he asked.

"No," growled Purvis, "Couple of 'em got nicked up a bit, they think, but none of 'em were killed."

"Professionals," said Lee.

"How the hell do ya know that?" barked Purvis.

Lee glanced over at Chacon and smiled. "An' he calls *you* an idiot."

Chacon laughed. This infuriated Purvis, who stormed across the room and slapped the young Mexican across the face hard.

"Ya don't never laugh at me, ya snot-nosed little shit!"

He turned to Lee. "The same goes for you an yer smart-ass mouth. Ya got that?"

Lee was beginning to understand what Frank had meant about being a dog.

"Hell, Bill. Think about it for a minute. Ya got four

men going up against eight. That's two-to-one odds, an' they kill all eight without losin' a man. Ya said it yerself. Poco an' his boys were top gunhands—an' they're all dead."

Chacon remained quiet, rubbing at the pain that still stung the right side of his face. For a fleeting second, he had almost drawn his gun to kill Bill Purvis right then and there. No man had ever put his hands on him and lived. Purvis was almost like a second father to him, but if he ever did that again, he was a dead man.

"That's damn bad luck for us," said Purvis. "We could have used Poco and his boys to side with us on this deal. If there's gonna be a fight with Notonte, I hate to show up shorthanded."

Setting his anger aside for the moment, Chacon said, "Why not find out if these four gringos would like to join us? If they are professionals as Lee says, they surely have a price for their services. Whatever that price might be would be well worth the money. They have already proven that four of them are as good as eight men."

Purvis thought about it for a moment. Chacon might have something there. Right now, he was surrounded by Mexicans, breeds, and a few Indians. Lee and Taggart were the only other Americans in the outfit. A few more gringos backing his play might not be a bad idea.

"Ya think ya can find 'em in two days?"

Chacon nodded and with confidence in his voice, replied, "We'll take Dog with us. He might be crazy, but he's a damn good tracker."

"Who else ya takin'?"

"Lee and Taggart and three or four of the other men."

Purvis was about to approve the plan when Dog appeared in the doorway. He spoke in broken English.

"Taggart. He gone. Take clothes—horse. He leave this place for good, I think."

The fury of earlier reappeared on the face of Bill Purvis.

"What? When?"

Dog shook his head. "No say. Men say he talk to Lee longhouse, then leave. This see Lee make bye-bye sign with hand."

Purvis was beside himself. In full fury now, Purvis turned on Lee.

"Ya knew the son of a bitch was gone all the time, didn't ya, ya lyin' bastard."

Mitch Lee stood his ground. "He didn't want no more part of it, Bill. What was I suppose to do, shoot him?"

"Ya goddamn right ya shoot him! Now we got a man ridin' around out there someplace, knows the where an' when of every damn thing we got goin' on in a couple of days."

Lee saw where this was going.

"Hellfire, Purvis. Frank ain't gonna say nothin' to no-body. He just wants to go back home to Texas, that's all. He didn't even care about the money. Said he was done with all this and wanted out. That's all."

Lee could see the veins in the man's neck begin to bulge. His face turned red and he puffed out his chest as he said, "He's done, all right! Dog, take some men with ya an' catch up to Taggart. He ain't been gone all that long so he can't have much of a lead. When ya find him—kill him!"

Dog showed a wide grin. Raising his hand to his ear, he began to make a sawing motion.

"Yeah, ya crazy bastard, ya can have his damn ears. Now get outta here." Mitch Lee drew his gun. Cocking the hammer back, he yelled for Dog to stay right where he was. Moving to the doorway, he motioned with the gun for Dog to join Chacon and Purvis by the desk.

"What the hell do you think you're doing, Lee?" asked Chacon.

Lee kept his gun leveled on the three men.

"I ain't rightly sure myself, amigo. I tried to talk Frank outta this, but he had his mind made up. Now, he ain't done nothin' to be gettin' killed for, an' that's a damn fact. He just wanted to get back to Texas, that's all. Now ya boys drop them guns and relax. Come on—unbuckle them gunbelts and let 'em fall."

As the gunbelts hit the floor, Purvis asked, "Just how long ya think ya can keep this up?"

"Long enough for Frank to put some miles between this place and the Rio. Hell, if I had any sense I'd 'a went with him, and took them two kids ya got locked up in there too. Now rest easy, boys. We're gonna be here a while."

Purvis, his face wild with rage, stared across the room at Lee. "Ya shoulda left with him, Lee. I'm gonna kill ya for this."

Lee only laughed. "That's big talk for a man lookin' down the barrel of a cocked .45, Bill. Now shut the hell up and set your ass down."

Moments earlier, Chacon had thought of trying to draw on Lee, but quickly put the idea out of his head. He realized he wouldn't have a chance. Besides, he was enjoying watching Big Bill Purvis having to follow orders from someone else for a change. Now if Lee would just come over and slap the hell out of Purvis, that would make this whole game worthwhile.

Ten minutes soon passed into thirty. Purvis began to

recant on his threat. If Lee trusted Frank not to talk, that
was now good enough for him. The threat had been made
in a fit of anger. He didn't really mean it. Hell, he was
already short of men. What was to be gained by killing
anybody else anyway? If Lee would put the gun away,
they'd all have a drink and forget about all this.

Lee saw that Purvis was trying hard to be convincing,
but the cowboy wasn't buying any of it. He had ridden
with this bunch long enough to know that Bill Purvis was
a lot of things, but a forgiving man wasn't one of them.

Standing off to the side of the doorway, Lee heard
someone coming up the steps and onto the porch.

"Not a word outta any of ya or I start shootin'."

A *vaquero* came walking through the door. Before the
man knew what happened, Lee had reached out and pulled
the man's gun from his holster. He shoved the man toward
the desk. There were more footsteps. Lee turned to glance
toward the doorway for a second. That was all it took.
The gunman felt a sudden sharp pain in the middle of his
back. He knew in an instant what it was. He could still
remember the stunned look on the face of the Covington
boy that day of the ranch raid, when Dog's knife had
suddenly appeared in his chest. Lee imagined that same
look was now on his own face. He'd forgotten about the
breed's blade. The same blade that in a few minutes
would be cutting his ears off. The room began to spin.
He slumped to the floor. There was the sound of scurrying
boots. He felt the knife being drawn slowly from his back.
The light began to fade, and there was a dull pain in the
left side of Mitch Lee's head as he drew his last breath.

Chacon ignored Dog, who was laughing as he went
about his grisly task.

"Do you still want us to go after Taggart?"

"No. I think Lee was right. He won't say anything."

"What about finding the four gringos?"

Purvis shook his head. He was disillusioned that the only two Americans in the outfit had turned against him. Chacon noted a hint of sadness in the big man's voice as he answered, "No. Never mind. We'll do this business with the men we have. At least I can trust them."

He started to yell at Dog to stop what he was doing, but it was already too late. The wild-eyed Comanche stood up holding one of Mitch Lee's ears in each hand and let out a war whoop. He then ran out the door and across the compound chanting like a madman.

"Get that damn body outta here an' send somebody up here to clean that blood off my floor."

Chacon reached down and placing his hands under Lee's arms, pulled the body out onto the porch. Purvis went back to his desk. Slumping down in his chair, he pulled a bottle of whiskey from a drawer. Taking a long pull on the bottle, he lowered it into his lap and stared at the blood-covered floor near the door.

"Maybe it's time I went home too," he muttered as he raised the bottle again.

ELEVEN

✦

"*BUENOS DIAS, SEÑOR* Dave. *Como está,* my friend?"

Don Ricardo Sanchez's greeting was a joyous one. The elderly man threw open his arms and hugged Dave Matther as if he were a long-lost son.

"*Bien*, Don Ricardo, *muy bien.*"

Don Ricardo Sanchez was fifty-nine years old. He wasn't a big man, but rather tall and slim. His hair was the color of faded silver, as were his mustache and a small goatee. Both were very well trimmed, presenting a gentlemanly appearance. The face was deeply tanned, showing the cracks and lines of a lifetime of hard work spent in the harsh Mexican climate.

"Don Ricardo, I would like you to meet my friends."

Dave introduced everyone, each receiving a hearty handshake and a smile as a warm welcome.

"Come, let us go into the shade of the veranda. We will have some wine while we talk. Miguel, take their horses to the water tank. I am sure they are in need of water. Come, my friends, this way."

They followed Sanchez to an elaborate covered patio with a huge round table in the center. Once they had settled comfortably into their chairs, servants began to bring out wine, along with fresh-baked bread and goat cheese. One brought out a tray of sliced melon and various other fruit. Sanchez noticed Pete take a sip of the wine and wrinkle his face as if he had just sucked a bad lemon. He motioned one of the women over and whispered something to her. A few minutes later, she returned with two bottles of fine bonded whiskey. Pete's eyes lit up and a smile broke across his crusty old face as he nodded his appreciation to Sanchez.

For the next few minutes, the men enjoyed the luxuries of these wonderful things found in such a far-away and isolated place. As was his habit, J.T. sipped at his wine while he studied his surroundings. The hacienda was larger than it appeared from the outside. Upon their arrival, they had been greeted by a three-foot-high adobe wall that surrounded the entire compound. Twenty-five to thirty yards from that wall was a second, higher wall. This one stood close to thirty feet high, with catwalks that ran all the way around on the inside, which would allow for men to fire from the top of the wall down into any attack force with relative safety.

To the south was the cannon Dave had told them about. It was an eight-pounder mounted on a reinforced parapet, its heavy barrel protruding through an opening cut in the top of the wall that would allow the gun to be swung 180 degrees from left to right and back again. It had been a tactically sound move to place the big gun on the south wall given the surrounding terrain. The south was the most logical and easiest avenue of approach for an attacker. At ground level, gun ports had also been cut in the wall at ten-foot intervals, which allowed for the men at these positions to cover not only a target directly to their front, but to the left and right on each side of them as well.

It was now clear to J.T. how Don Ricardo had managed to withstand the constant attacks from bandits and Indians over the years. The hacienda was a veritable fort capable of holding off an entire army. In the rear of the place were the stables and a corral that could easily hold up to a hundred horses. A separate corral contained cattle. To the right of that was a bellows with all the equipment needed for a smithy. Two longhouses served as bunkhouses for the single men, while small two- and three-room adobe homes were for the married men and their families. There was even a small chapel with a bell tower that served as a lookout tower. If there was trouble headed their way, the man in the tower would ring the bell sounding the call to arms. All in all, it wasn't a place J.T. would want to try and take in a battle, no matter how big an army he had backing him.

"So tell me, my friend, what brings you and your compadres to our mountains?" asked Sanchez.

Dave retold the story of the Comanchero raid on the Covington home and the kidnapping of the two children. As Dave told of the fate of the children, J.T. saw the sadness come into Sanchez's face. Don Ricardo expressed his sympathies to Abe, telling him that he was not alone in his pain. Untold numbers of Mexican people had suffered a similar fate at the hands of the dreaded Comancheros. Men killed, women and children carried away, never to be seen again. The Comancheros were truly a curse upon the land. Of that there was no doubt.

Abe set his glass down as he said, "Don Ricardo, these murderers have to have a place from which to operate. Do you have any idea where that headquarters might be located?"

Don Ricardo was silent for a moment as he pondered the question, then answered, "You ask a difficult question, my friend. I have lived most of my life in the shadows of these mountains, yet there remain places that even I have not traveled. Three times I have taken my men out in search of these Comancheros. We sought to find them and destroy them in their lair, but each time we have returned empty-handed."

"Juan believes that these men may be hiding in an area called the Chomais Pass," said J.T.

Sanchez raised an eyebrow. "Yes, that is a very good choice. I have searched there before, but for only a short distance. It could be that they are hiding farther back in the pass. There are many arroyos and caves in that part of the mountains. We have only searched a few. It is possible one may lead to an unknown passage. I cannot say that this is so. I can only offer possibilities. I am sorry."

Abe sat back in his chair, his face showing both worry and disappointment. J.T. was about to ask another question when the bell suddenly began to ring. Don Ricardo was on his feet and running for the chapel before the others had even made it out of their chairs.

"What's going on, Dave?" asked J.T.

"Trouble!" shouted Matther as he broke into a run for the courtyard.

Before the men reached the chapel, the sound of gunfire

could be heard in the distance. Sanchez called up to his men in the bell tower. *"Qué pasa?"*

One of the excited men yelled, "Apaches!"

The other lookout rattled off something in rapid-fire Spanish, so fast that the Americans understood only part of what he was saying. Don Ricardo turned to his guests.

"Apaches are in pursuit of a lone rider. He is trying to reach the hacienda. We can see from the wall. Come, follow me."

The men scrambled up the stairs to the catwalk. In the distance, they saw the single rider, his big bay running at full stride. Behind him, a wide cloud of dust rose from thirty or forty Apaches who were slowly, but surely, closing the distance on their prey.

"He'll never make it," said Billy Tyler. "His horse looks like he's about to cave in. See how he's already flattening in the stride?"

"That horse goes down, that fella's a dead man," said Harvey.

Don Ricardo told his men to take aim with their rifles. Once the Apaches were in range, he would give the order to fire. J.T. wasn't going to wait. He turned and rushed down the steps.

"Where the hell is he goin'?" asked Matt.

Sanchez looked back over his shoulder. Seeing J.T. running for the water tank, he knew where the bounty hunter was going. He shouted to his men below, "Open the gates!"

Pulling a .45 from his saddlebags, J.T. stuck the extra gun in his waistband, then was in the saddle and racing for the gates, nearly riding down the *vaqueros* pushing the heavy doors open. They scurried out of the way as J.T. rode out. From above, he heard a volley of rifle fire

suddenly erupt from the wall. Sanchez had given the order
to fire. J.T. saw four Apaches knocked from their horses.
Pulling the gun from his waist with one hand and drawing
the other from his holster, J.T. leaned forward in the saddle and charged forward, firing with a gun in each hand.
It was reminiscent of his days as a guerrilla fighter during
the war when he had ridden with Bloody Bill Anderson.

"Would ya look at that," said Harvey as he and the men
on the wall watched in stunned amazement as more
Apaches began to fall.

For a brief moment, it looked as if the bay would carry
its rider to safety. J.T. wheeled Toby around as the man
came abreast of him. "Ride for your life!" shouted J.T. as
both men raced for the open gates, still five hundred yards
away, with rifle and pistol fire providing what cover it
could from the wall.

Two hundred yards short of the gates, J.T. heard a bullet strike meat. The bay whinnied, threw its head back,
and stumbled, pitching his rider over the horse's head to
land rolling in the dirt like a tumbleweed.

J.T. pulled rein, swung his horse around, and rode
straight for the man, who was now on his feet. "Your
arm!" J.T. yelled.

The man holstered his gun and put his arm out, grabbing J.T.'s hand as he rode by. Pulling hard, J.T. swung
the man up behind him, wheeled his horse again, and
broke for the safety of the hacienda gates as bullets tore
out chunks of adobe wall and sent splinters flying from
the heavy wooden doors.

As they rode into the courtyard, the gates were quickly
closed behind them. There was a pause in the firing from
the hacienda as those inside sent up a loud cheer. Their
quarry lost, the Apaches broke off and began heading

back to the west, stopping to pick up their dead along the way.

Abe and the others came down from the wall and gathered around J.T. and the man who owed his life to the bounty hunter. J.T. rubbed and patted Toby's neck as he watched the man he had just saved dust himself off. He seemed to be all right. It was then that J.T. noticed the rig the man was wearing. The holster and gunbelt were black in color and made of top-grade leather. The initials "FT" were hand-tooled on the side of the tied-down holster. Even after his spill into the dirt, the Colt .45 Peacemaker he carried looked as new as the day it had been made. A master craftsman always took care of his tools. J.T. didn't know who the man was, but he recognized the telltale signs of a gunfighter when he saw them.

"You all in one piece, mister?" asked J.T.

Frank Taggart looked up. "Wouldn't be if it wasn't for you, friend."

Reaching out his hand, he continued. "Name's Frank Taggart. I owe you, mister. Thanks."

Recognizing the name, J.T. took the extended hand in a firm grip. "I've heard of you, Taggart. You downed the two Comacho brothers in a gunfight in El Paso earlier this year. That right?"

"That's right. They didn't give me much choice. Braced me when I was leadin' my horse out of the livery stable. Told 'em I didn't want no trouble, but they wanted to push it—that got 'em killed."

"Wasn't there a poster on them Comacho boys, J.T.?" asked Billy.

Before John Law could reply, Taggart muttered, "J.T.? You wouldn't happen to be J.T. Law, the bounty man, would ya?"

"I would."

Taggart grinned. "Heard of you too."

Pete had been slow coming down the stairs. As he pushed his way through the crowd around the two men, he saw Taggart.

"Well, cut my whiskers an' call me naked, if it ain't Frank Taggart."

Taggart's grin widened when he saw Pete Simmons.

"Well, I'll be damn. Pete, how the hell are ya? Last I heard, Ol' Judge Parker was linin' ya up for the long drop. Some said ya was already dead."

Pete grinned through broken, tobacco-stained teeth. "Hell, Frank. I done heard that so many times, even I'm startin' to believe I'm dead. Folks said ya come down south after that Paso business. Damn good seein' ya again."

Taggart glanced at the faces that surrounded him. "Damn, boys, I ain't seen this many gringos all together in one place since I been down here. What brings you fellas to ol' Mexico?"

"We'll talk about that in a while. First I want you to meet everybody." Law made the introductions all around. Taggart was especially grateful to Don Ricardo for the safety of his hacienda, and told him so. By the time J.T. had finished, Taggart, like Matther earlier, appeared confused by the makeup of the company he now found himself in. He knew Pete, of course, and had heard of the ex-lawman Dave Matther. But he knew nothing about the McMasters brothers, and was totally taken by surprise when the bounty hunter introduced Abe and Billy as Texas Rangers. It was a strange mix of characters, there was no doubt about that.

Don Ricardo sent his people back to work while the

Americans retired to the patio. Taggart, his mouth as dry as cotton, downed a half a bottle of wine, then chased it with a shot of whiskey. There was a few minutes of small talk, then Pete asked, "Where were you headed when those Apaches jumped ya, Frank?"

Taggart poured another glass of whiskey, but sipped on it this time.

"Was headin' for the Rio, then on home to Arizona. Figured that El Paso business had cooled down by now. Run into them red devils a few miles out from Chomais Pass."

Suddenly, all conversation at the table stopped. Taggart found every eye on him. The gunfighter knew he'd said something wrong, but didn't know what it was. J.T., his elbows on the table, leaned forward and looked Taggart in the eyes.

"You were coming out of Chomais Pass?"

Taggart could feel the tension around him. All the eyes were on him, but none looked as threatening as those of the Ranger called Abe. Then it hit him—Covington. John Law had said the man's name was Abe Covington. Taggart's mind flashed back to the little girl they had carried off. She had said her name was Covington—Debbie Covington. The Ranger leaned closer. There was no doubting the threatening tone of Abe's voice.

"Answer the question, Taggart. Were you coming out of Chomais Pass?"

Taggart downed his drink, then sleeved his mouth with his shirt. Like sunlight bursting through during a rainstorm, everything was suddenly clear to the gunfighter. All the gringos were here for one reason and one reason only—to save the Covington children. He had escaped from one bunch of hostiles into the waiting arms of another bunch that would more than likely kill him when they heard he had ridden with the raiding party that day. This time there was no place to run. The cards had been dealt and from the looks of things, it was a losing hand and time to pay up.

Pete had known Taggart for a time, and he was a friend. He didn't care for Abe's tone of voice, or John Law's either, for that matter. Taggart had done a lot of things, but riding with Comancheros was about as low as a man could get. That wasn't the Frank Taggart he knew, and he told them so.

"Now hold on here, fellas," Pete said. "Just 'cause a man happens on a place don't mean he's part of nothin'. I knowed Frank here for a good spell an' I'd stake my name that he—"

Taggart reached over and put his hand on the old man's shoulder, cutting him off.

"Don't do that, Pete."

"But Frank," he stammered, "these fellows is thinkin' ya mighta been hooked up with them damn Comancheros we're lookin' for."

Taggart patted his old friend on the shoulder. "That's all right, Pete."

Looking across the table, Taggart met John Law's stare head-on when he spoke.

"Come down here after those two kids, didn't ya?"

Abe was across the table and had Taggart by the front of the shirt before anyone could grab him.

"You no-good son of a bitch! You're one of 'em that helped kill my brother and his wife. I'm gonna tear you apart with my bare hands, Taggart."

"Somebody grab Abe!" shouted J.T. as he hurried around the table and pulled Taggart's gun from his holster, then jerked the gunman out of Abe's grip and away from the table. Pete didn't move. The sadness and disappointment were written on his weathered face. In the meantime, it took all the others to hold the Ranger captain down.

"All right—that's enough! Settle down, Abe, goddamnit! This man is the only one that can lead us to those two kids. Now stop it or I'll have you hogtied! I mean it."

His initial rage slowly fading, Abe nodded and stopped resisting. Pouring himself a drink, he stared across at Taggart.

"Have you seen the kids?"

Taggart looked back over his shoulder. "You can let go now. You got my gun an' I'm not goin' anywhere."

J.T. released the man's arms and told him to sit down. From the looks he was receiving from the men around him, Taggart felt he would have been better off if the Apaches had killed him. J.T. sat down beside him.

"Okay, Taggart, tell us about it. Where are the kids?"

Taggart couldn't look at Pete, or any of the others, either. He focused his eyes on a cut in the table and with his head down, began.

"The kids were fine last time I saw 'em. Outfit's run by Big Bill Purvis and Pablo Chacon. Figure they got fifty, maybe sixty guns ridin' with 'em."

"Where are they holed up?"

"Chomais Pass. About two miles back. It's a son of a bitch to find if ya don't know what to look for. Got a good-size compound in there. Corrals, main house, bunkhouses. Got quite a few women and kids in there too."

"Well, what the hell we waitin' for?" said Billy. "Let's ride."

Some of the men started to rise.

"That's a bad idea, kid," said Taggart. "Ya got about two hours of daylight left. It'll take most of that just to get to the pass. Be dark by the time ya got halfway up the arroyo. Ya don't wanta be stumblin' around out there in the dark. Trust me. Some of then drop-offs are a hundred feet straight down. Then there's the guards. Ya'll have to get by three of 'em, an' they're goin' be above ya lookin' down. An' that's all before ya even see the compound. It's gonna be a tough nut to crack, boys. Take my word for it. Then there's the Apaches."

"Apaches," said Matt. "Here we go again with the damn Apaches. What the hell they got to do with this, Taggart?"

Taggart seemed surprised by the question. Then he thought about it for a moment.

"You boys must have left Texas before the news got out."

"What news?" asked J.T.

"Purvis got some information from a man in Laredo about a shipment of new Winchesters and ammo being transported by the Army. We ambushed 'em in Casa Blanco Pass, killed the troopers, and took the wagons. Purvis has worked up a deal with Notonte, the Apache war chief. Gold for the rifles and ammo. Notonte's had a month to get the gold together. The exchange is supposed to happen day after tomorrow."

"Son of a bitch!" said Abe. "That's why we saw the buzzards the day we crossed the Rio. Those Indians get their hands on those new Winchesters and they'll be across the border into Texas raidin' and killin' before the week's out. It'll be like the Comanche wars all over again."

J.T. could sense that Taggart was holding something back.

"What else, Taggart? What is it you're not telling us?"

Taggart raised his eyes from the table for the first time. With sad eyes, he looked across the table at Abe. "I'm sorry, Captain. I really am. If I'd known what he was going to do with those kids, I'd have never let it happen."

"What are you talkin' about?" asked Abe.

"Along with the rifles and bullets, he's gonna throw the kids in as a present to Notonte."

Abe went into a rage again, leaping for Taggart, but being pulled back by the powerful hands of Harvey McMasters, who said, "Now, Abe, this ain't doin' nobody no good an' ya know it. So just set down like Mr. Law said."

"So you're sayin' we can't get there now. We're goin' have to wait for mornin', that right?" asked John Law.

Taggart sat back in his chair. "Like I said, Law, it's a damn dangerous place at night. An' two miles is a long way to travel in the dark. Honest, if I thought ya had any chance in hell of gettin' them kids outta there tonight, I'd tell ya so."

Pete finally looked at Taggart.

"How'd ya ever get mixed up with that bunch anyway, Frank?"

Everyone was quiet. It was a question that had been on all their minds, especially John Law's.

Taggart told them that after the El Paso shootout with the Comacho Brothers, some of their friends had tried to ambush him. In a running gun battle he had crossed the border into Mexico with seven men in hot pursuit. They'd finally managed to corner him in a small arroyo, and were closing in on him when Mitch Lee and Bill Purvis showed up with some of the Comancheros. They made short work of the seven men, killing all of them. They then asked Taggart to join up with them. Feeling that he owed them for getting him out of the fix he was in, he went along for two reasons. He was a good gunhand, and there was safety in numbers. The Comacho boys had a lot of friends. At first, it hadn't been so bad. Most of the fighting had been against other bandits and renegade Indians. But then had come the raid on the Covington ranch.

It wasn't something he was proud of. That was clear by the painful look on the gunfighter's face as he told his story. He said that was when he should have left the outfit right then and there, but he had become close friends with Mitch Lee, and the exchange with Notonte was going to put a fair amount of money in their pockets, so he had let himself be talked into staying around. When he found out that Purvis planned to turn the kids over to the Apaches, that was more than he could take. He told the men around the table that he had even entertained the idea of trying to get the kids out of there himself. He didn't know if they believed him, but whether they did or not, it was the truth. He had been toying with the idea while cleaning his guns that morning. Now he was glad he hadn't tried anything. If he had by some miracle gotten them out with him, they'd be in the hands of the Apaches right now and he'd be dead. There was no way the kids could have kept up during the chase.

All in all, it had worked out for the best. He finished by telling the men that his decision to join the Comancheros, no matter how obligated he might have felt at the time, had been a bad one, no doubt about that. If he could somehow go back and change it, he would. But he couldn't. No amount of wishing or praying was going to change anything now. He was ready to stand up for his mistake and take whatever punishment the men deemed necessary. If it was to be a hanging, then so be it.

Taggart's story and his strong forthright admission of wrongdoing had given pause to many at the table. He'd made no excuses and asked for no quarter for his error in judgment. That said a lot about the man.

"We ain't gonna hang anybody, Taggart," said J.T. "Hell, you're our only way into that place. That is, if you're willing to lead us in there."

Taggart nodded. "Nothin' would give me more pleasure, John Law."

Abe was bitter, and still had the killer look in his eye.

"How the hell ya know ya can trust this son of a bitch not to warn his pals?"

Taggart's voice was calm, and his words rang true with sincerity.

"Mr. Covington, I am sorry about your brother and his family. There's nothing I can do to change what happened that day. But I swear to you on my mother's grave, I'll do whatever it takes to get those two kids out of there. It wouldn't change what's already happened, but it's my chance to right a wrong that I was a part of. All I can do is give you my word. That's all I got left."

Dave Matther nodded as he said, "As a lawman, I've always looked a man in the eye when he told me anything. You do it long enough, you get to where you can tell when a man's lyin'. I don't see that here."

"Me neither," said Pete. "Even after all this other business, I'd take Frank Taggart's word over many a so-called honest man anytime."

J.T. saw the tough gunman's lower lip quiver slightly

as he looked at his old friend and muttered, "Thanks, Pete."

J.T. looked around the group. "What about the rest of you boys? You feel the same way? After all, it's gonna be your asses on the line out there. If you got any objections, now's the time to speak up."

Harvey and Matt looked at each other. Harvey nodded. "We got no problem with it, J.T. Ain't a man here ain't took a wrong step somewhere in his life."

Billy agreed. He didn't have a problem with it either. "How about you, J.T.?" he asked.

John Thomas Law figured he had taken more wrong steps in his life than any man there. He'd ridden with men considered outcasts during the war, robbed banks with the James boys. Lost his girl and become a falling-down drunk because of it. No, he was the last man in the world to condemn Frank Taggart for making poor decisions. He figured he had become a pretty good judge of men over the last few years. Watching Taggart as he had told his story, J.T. had been convinced that the hardened gunfighter was still troubled over the raid on the Covington ranch and the taking of the children. He was only asking for a chance to redeem himself, not only in the eyes of the men at the table, but the eyes of God as well.

"I say we can trust him."

Abe stood up. Harvey started to grab him again. "No need for that, Harvey. Ya all done made it clear how ya feel. I'll go along with it." Leaning on the table, Abe stared hard at Taggart. "But you remember this, Frank Taggart. We ain't done. Not by a long shot. This things over—I'm gonna kill you."

J.T. turned to the Ranger. "Abe. I want your word. There won't be no trouble between you two until this thing is over an' we're got those kids back across the Rio. Can you give me your word and keep it, mister?"

"You got my word."

"How about you, Taggart?" asked J.T.

The gunfighter held out his hands and pointed to his empty holster. "Don't think I'm much of a threat, Law. I got no gun."

J.T. pulled the well-oiled .45 from his belt and tossed it to Taggart.

"Now you're heeled. Have I got your word?"

"Yes, sir, you do."

"Good. Then set down here an' let's figure out how we're gonna do this."

TWELVE

✶

PLANNING THE ATTACK on the Comanchero camp had lasted late into the night. Don Ricardo had gone among his people at the hacienda and asked for volunteers to join with the Americans in their fight with the bandits. He'd asked that only single men volunteer. Fifteen brave men had stepped forward. It was welcome news to J.T., who thanked each one for his courage and commitment.

The fact that Taggart knew the exact positions of the sentries would allow for the element of surprise. Once they were taken care of, they would be replaced by Don Ricardo's men. J.T. and the others would move down to the outer fringes of the camp. Billy Tyler, Harvey, and Pete would remain in positions halfway down the mountain and provide cover fire with their rifles if things went bad. Dave Matther and Juan would take some men and circle around and come in from the west. Matt and Abe, with their group, would go around to the east side of the camp, while J.T. and Taggart worked their way toward the front gates. No one was to fire unless it was absolutely necessary.

The key to the whole plan was surprise. J.T. and Taggart hoped, by using their knives, that they could silently get the kids out of the compound before anyone knew what was happening. But if the element of surprise should be lost, they hoped to get to the kids in the confusion that was sure to follow once the shooting started. Either way, the kids were the important thing. They had to get them outside the compound to have any chance of escape. They would rather have located the kids, then waited until dark to make their move, but as Taggart had said, escaping in the dark was nearly impossible, not to mention deadly. It would have to be done in broad daylight, during the afternoon siesta. Their plans completed, the men set about cleaning their weapons for the work that lay ahead.

J.T. saw Taggart sitting by himself against a wall, smoking a cigarette and staring up at the stars.

"Mind if I join you?"

Taggart shook his head. "If ya don't mind settin' next to a leper, it's fine with me."

J.T. laughed, then slid down next to the gunfighter and rolled a smoke.

"Not much company comin' by to chat, huh, Frank?"

"Naw, but that's understandable, I reckon."

J.T. lit his roll and blew out a long stream of smoke. "How old are you, Frank?"

Taggart thought that was a strange question, but was glad for the conversation.

"Thirty-five."

"You see any time in the war?"

"Yeah, with the Texas Brigade. We was with Hood at Second Bull Run an' at bloody Antietam. Went into the war a cocky twenty-one-year-old. Thought I knew what it was all about. Got sick before the first battle I was ever in. God, that was a damn terrible war."

J.T. stared off in the distance as he replied, "Yeah, it was. Sometimes, it seems like it was just yesterday. Other times, I feel like it was all a dream an' I was standin' back watchin' the whole thing. Don't seem real, you know what I mean? You said the Texas Brigade. I thought you were from Arizona."

"Naw. I was born in Texas. Headed to Arizona after the war. Liked the country up there and just stayed. Even got married. Didn't last long, though. I was still young. Couldn't get that damn war outta my mind. Started drinkin' too much and slappin' her around like it was all her fault. She left me. Smartest thing that girl ever done."

J.T. flipped his smoke out in front of him and shifted positions against the wall.

"Wanta ask you somethin', Frank. Who cut the ears off those boys at the ranch?"

Taggart spat to the side, then answered, "A goddamn half-breed Comanche called Dog. Been with Purvis a long time, from what I gathered. Bastard's as crazy as a bedbug. Collects ears. Keeps 'em on a string he carries around his saddlehorn. Don't know how he stands it. Damn things stink to high heaven. Always got that smell of death around him. But he's a damn dangerous man, John Law. Can track a mouse over a mountain. Crack shot with a rifle and even more dangerous with a knife. Keeps one hid in a sheath that hangs on his back under his vest. You ever come up on him, watch for that. If I don't kill nobody else in this deal, I wanta kill that damn breed."

"You just might get that chance, Frank. I'll see you in the mornin', got to get some sleep."

John Law stood up, and was about to leave when Taggard said, "Hey, Law."

J.T. turned around and looked down at him.

"Thanks for givin' me a second chance."

J.T. grinned. "I don't know, Frank. That second chance just might get you killed tomorrow."

"Yeah, well, at least I'll be fightin' on the right side this time. Night, John Law."

PURVIS WAS AS nervous as a whore in church. Five of Notonte's warriors had showed up at the gate. The chief had sent them to inspect the rifles and to make sure that they were all there along with the ammunition. Chacon had taken them to the wagons, opened a box, and pulled out five of the brand-new rifles, handing one to each brave along with three bullets each. He showed them how to load the guns, then taking one himself, fired three rapid shots at a tree on the side of the mountain. All three shots tore bark. He then motioned for the five braves to do the same. Like children with a new toy, the braves fired their three shots, then shouted with excitement as they caressed the new weapons.

It hadn't taken much convincing. One of the men started to take the rifles back, but Chacon, always the smart businessman, told him to let the braves have them. They could take them back to show Notonte. They were a gift. He gave each warrior a box of bullets and sent them on their way.

Purvis had watched the transaction from his position on

the porch. When he saw the Indians ride off with the rifles, he started to signal the guards at the gates to stop them, but it was too late. They were already out of the compound and headed for the mountains. What the hell was Chacon thinking giving away his damn rifles like that? Five rifles—that was over five hundred dollars that had just ridden out that gate. He had half a mind to have the damn upstart tied to the whipping post and take five hundred dollars worth of hide off his back. He would have too, if he wasn't so short of men. He couldn't afford to lose any more. A reckless act like that right now could turn a lot of the *vaqueros* against him. Maybe later, after this business with the Apaches was over.

Chacon came walking up to the house. He could see the big man was upset by his wrinkled brow and hard-set jaw. There was a time when that would have worried the young Mexican bandit, but not now. Purvis was the only gringo with the Comancheros. True, he had ridden with Chacon's father and been his right-hand man for years, but that was another time. It was Chacon's father who had formed this band of Comancheros. It was time the heir to that leadership position took his rightful place.

"What the hell ya think yer doin' givin' my damn rifles away, ya little son of a bitch?"

Chacon smiled. "Oh, so now those are your rifles, that right, Bill?"

"Ya goddamn right they are. I'm the one set this whole damn thing up. That makes 'em my rifles. It's me No-tonte'll deal with, an' don't ya forget it. My rifles, my deal, an' my gold to split any way I see fit. An' the way I see it now, ya done cut yer share by five hundred dollars by givin' them guns away."

Chacon motioned to three vaqueros who had followed

him from the gate. They moved up to the hitch rail in front of the house. Chacon walked up the steps to the porch. As he placed himself only a few feet in front of Purvis, a sly grin began to spread across his face.

"I think maybe it is you that have lost, Bill. And a lot more than just rifles. My new Apache friends brought a message from Notonte. It would appear he no longer trusts you. He prefers to deal with the son of the man they had trusted for years. The son of the great Comanchero Hector Chacon. Out of respect for the friendship between you and my father, I will give you one hour to gather your things and leave this place."

Bill Purvis took a step back. His face began to take on a flushed look. The veins in his neck began to swell and pulsate as the uncontrollable anger rose within him. He knew he should have killed this little son of a bitch when he had the chance. Now the little shit had the balls to think he could just up and take over. Well, he was wrong.

Bill's big hands shot out and grabbed the young man's shirt. Holding tight and pulling him forward with one, he slapped Chacon hard across the face with the back of the other.

"Why, ya little pissant. I'm gonna beat yer ass till—"

Purvis heard a shot. Felt a burning pain rip at his stomach. His eyes were wide with surprise, as if he was trying to understand what had just happened. Where had the shot come from? Why did his gut hurt so bad? He looked down and saw Chacon's pistol pressed against his shirt. Could smell the smoldering cloth of the shirt and the sick-sweet scent of burning flesh. He began to lose the grip in his hand as it slowly slid away from Chacon's shirt. He looked up into the eyes of the boy he had raised from a kid. He opened his mouth to ask why, but the word was

drowned out by the loud sound of another bullet being
fired into his stomach. Bill Purvis staggered back, his
bloody shirt on fire. In a final desperate effort, he reached
for his gun, but before he could pull it from the holster,
the roar of four guns sent a flurry of bullets into his body,
driving him back against the wall. The firing continued
long after Big Bill Purvis was dead.

Chacon reloaded his pistol as he stood over the body.
Looking down at the bloody mess that lay before him, he
said, "I gave you a chance to leave, you old fool. Now
look what you've made me do."

The three *vaqueros* came up onto the porch. Removing
their hats, they waited for instructions from their new
leader.

"Take him to where my father is buried. Place him in
the ground next to him. It is only right. They once rode
together, now they shall rest beside each other."

Chacon walked into the house. Moving to the large
desk, he swung the leather chair around and sat down. At
last, he was where he should be. He would broker the
deal with the Apaches, thus gaining a valuable ally while
acquiring a fortune in gold with which to strengthen his
empire. Before long, everyone would know the name
Pablo Chacon.

In the back bedroom of the house, Debbie saw a woman
come into the room. There was an excitement in her voice
as she told the woman watching over them something in
hurried Spanish. Although not fluent in the language,
Debbie understood enough to know that something had
happened to Bill Purvis and that Pablo Chacon was now
in charge. That explained all the shooting they had heard
earlier. For a brief moment, fourteen-year-old Debbie
found new hope. Perhaps he would even let them go. But

that all changed when the door opened and she saw Pablo standing in the door.

The man motioned for the women to leave the room. They looked at one another, then to the young girl, who now set on the bed, her hands tied behind her back. They saw the lustful look in Chacon's eyes, and felt a sudden pity and sadness for the gringo girl.

"Get out, I said! An' take the boy out with you."

Making the sign of the cross, the women hurried across the room. Grabbing up young Thomas, they scurried from the bedroom, closing the door behind them.

Debbie tried to stand and run to the other side of the room, but Chacon reached out and grabbing the front of her dress, threw her back onto the bed. Fear gripped her very soul as she watched the man take off his gunbelt, then remove his shirt. As he began to take off his pants, she turned away, hiding her face in the corner. Tears began to flow as she heard him cross the room and felt the bed sag as he sat down beside her. She felt his fingers undoing the buttons on the back of her dress. Felt a hand move down inside the front of the dress and touch her young breasts.

Chacon's breath was hot against her ear as he leaned against her and whispered, "You are too tender a present to be given away. I will keep you for my pleasure."

Her eyes tightly closed, she felt the clothes fall away from her body as he untied her hands and placed her lengthwise on the bed. As he crawled on top of her, Debbie tried to think of a far-away place, of her mother and the fun they had had together.

A haunting scream of terror and pain rose from the house. The women on the front porch placed their hands over Thomas's ears and took the little boy away.

THIRTEEN

✦

As DAWN PUSHED its way along the horizon, the daily activities of the Sanchez hacienda had already begun. Smoke rose from the stovepipe of the large kitchen as the cooks began to prepare breakfast. Don Ricardo had offered the Americans the accommodations of his home. They'd thanked him, but had preferred to sleep out under the stars.

For many of the men, it had been a restless night. Especially for Abe Covington. The Ranger's attempts at sleep had been constantly interrupted by terrifying visions of Debbie and Thomas suffering at the hands of the Comancheros. At one point during the night, when he had finally managed to fall asleep, he swore he heard Debbie scream his name and cry out for help. It had seemed so real that Abe had bolted upright from his bedroll with his gun in his hand. Only to find himself staring out into the silent darkness.

Now, at the first hint of dawn, he moved along the line of bedrolls, tapping the toe of his boot against the men still bundled up in their blankets and telling them it was time to get up. When he came to the end of the line, he nudged John Law until he woke up.

"Come on, J.T. It's comin' up dawn. Let's get started."

J.T. sat up. Rubbing the sleep from his eyes, he stretched his arms over his head. Looking over to the side wall of the hacienda, he saw there was no one there.

"Where's Taggart?" he asked.

Abe, in a near panic at the thought that the man might had escaped them, drew his gun as John Law scrambled out of his blankets.

"You fellas lookin' for me?"

Abe and J.T. whirled around to find Frank Taggart sitting astride a big chestnut bay Don Ricardo had provided him. Taggart was already packed up and ready to ride. Leaning forward, he crossed his arms on the pommel of his saddle as he said, "Thought you boys wanted to get after the Comancheros. You boys gonna sleep all mornin', or can we get started?"

J.T. showed a halfway grin as he nodded. Frank Taggart had given his word and he was trying to show the value of that word. If he had wanted, he could have been gone before they ever woke up. Any doubts J.T. might have had about the man disappeared at that moment. Abe, however, was still not convinced that they could trust him. The bitterness was still there as he put his gun away.

"You had a chance to save yourself, Taggart. At least ya ain't a damn coward. I'll have to give ya that much. But it don't change nothin' between us."

"Didn't expect it would, Ranger. I'll be waitin' for you boys down by the gate. Best we get movin'. That sun's gonna be plenty hot today."

As Taggart turned away and rode to the main gate, Abe turned to J.T.

"Ya like the bastard, don't ya?"

J.T. shrugged his shoulders. "I gotta respect any man that admits his mistakes and is willing to die to make things right. This thing don't work out today, you got any idea what those Comancheros will do to Taggart if they get their hands on him alive? Well, I figure he's thought about it plenty. But you notice he's the first one ready to ride this morning. That says a lot about the man. You oughta think about that, Abe."

Twenty minutes later, they were ready to ride. Seeing that the men were not going to take the time to wait for breakfast, Sanchez had biscuits and jerky wrapped in towels, which were gratefully accepted by the men. Don Ricardo wished them Godspeed as they wheeled their horses about and headed for the main gates. Frank Taggart took the lead, with J.T. and Abe right behind him. The darkness gave way to the sun as it started its climb in the morning sky.

Three hours in the saddle brought them to the base of the mountain that led to the entrance of the Chomais Pass. It wasn't even noon yet, and already the heat was stifling. Motioning toward a cut between a stand of mesquite and black brush, Taggart led out, again heading east. Once through the brush, they dropped down into an arroyo and turned back north toward the mountain, working their way up the arroyo, through mesquite, catclaw, and prickly pear that grabbed at their pants legs. As they climbed higher, the trail became easier. J.T. estimated they had gone nearly two miles up the arroyo when Taggart raised his hand, stopping the group. J.T. eased Toby up beside him.

"What is it, Taggart?"

Taggart nodded up toward a peak to the right of the trail. "First sentry is posted just on the other side of that peak on the right. Somebody's gonna have to climb up this side and circle around to get him. We crest that ridge up ahead, he'll see us for sure."

J.T. dropped back and told the others. Juan volunteered to make the climb. Another *vaquero* would make the climb with him. Once the sentry was dead, the *vaquero* would put on the dead man's shirt and hat so as not to raise the suspicions of the other sentries stationed on the other peaks farther into the canyon. Taggart reminded the men that if there was a single shot, they would never get close to that compound. Stepping down from his horse and pulling out his knife, Juan nodded that he understood. As the men watched Juan and the *vaquero* make their way up through the outcropping of rocks, J.T. looked to Dave Matther.

"What'd you think, Dave? Can he do it?"

"Put your money on him every time, John T. He's quiet as a cat and damn deadly with that knife."

They watched the two men climb for fifteen minutes. Then they disappeared from sight as they moved around to the other side of the peak. Tensions were high as each minute in the heat made it seem like hours. Thirty minutes passed. Then Harvey pointed up. Juan was coming down the side of the mountain. He waved that the way was clear. Above him, the *vaquero* waved them forward.

Matther led Juan's horse up the arroyo, Juan meeting them at the top of the ridge. There was blood on the collar of his shirt.

"Are you hurt?" asked his friend.

"Not mine," said Juan.

A few hundred yards up, Taggart stopped them again and pointed to a high ridge on the left. Again Juan and a *vaquero* dismounted and began to climb. The others didn't have to wait long for the signal this time. The slant of the ridge had made the climb easier for the two men. Again, Juan rejoined them, and they moved forward. Taggart told them there was only one outpost left. It was farther in and could be seen from the compound. Thirty minutes later, Juan returned. They had managed to silence all three sentries and replace them with their own men. So far, everything was going well. But getting through a pass and getting into a compound full of people without being noticed was going to be a hell of a lot harder.

The group gathered at the top of a ridge and stared down into the Comanchero camp. Taggart began to point out locations. The longhouses where most of the men bunked. The corral and barn, and nearby the five wagons with the rifles and ammunition. The kitchen and the main house. The camp was bigger than any of them had figured. The mere size of the camp was going to make moving about a risky business at best. At the main gate, there were two guards, both with rifles.

Backing away from the ridge, the men sat around in a circle as J.T. drew a likeness of what they had just seen in the dirt. Again, they began to go over the plan. When it came to who was going to provide rifle fire from the side of the ridge, Pete ask J.T. to reconsider using him as one of the men.

"Hell, son. I ain't no good with a long gun. Shotgun's my choice every time. An' from the looks of that place down there, yer gonna be needin' a street howitzer. Es-

pecially if any shootin' starts. Hell, they'll be folks runnin' all over the place. Ya'll be needin' a scattergun.
What's ya say?"

J.T. looked to Abe. The Ranger agreed. Two riflemen
would be enough to cover the compound from above.
They were going to need more help inside the camp if
things went bad, and a shotgun was a great equalizer. The
others agreed. Billy and Harvey would handle the cover
fire, while Pete would join up with Matther's group,
which would come in from the west. The final details of
the plan complete, the men tried to find someplace out of
the sun to rest. It was a little before eleven o'clock. Siesta
time was normally between one and three. J.T. and Abe
would keep watch on the camp. When they felt the time
was right, the group would make their move.

J.T. figured the heat at somewhere near a hundred degrees at straight-up noon. Sweat beaded his face as he
watched the coming and going of the men below through
a spyglass. He had searched every part of the compound
with the glass. Somewhere down there amid those killers
and cutthroats were two frightened children who had had
their world turned upside down. But as bad as they may
have felt their situation was now, it was nothing compared
to what awaited them tomorrow. J.T. and the others realized that if their rescue effort should fail, the real nightmare for the two kids would begin when they were turned
over to the Apaches.

J.T. could only imagine how hard this waiting must be
for his friend Abe. Lying there next to him in the hot sun,
knowing that the men he was watching were the same
men that had slaughtered his brother and his family. That
somewhere down there a fourteen-year-old girl and a ten-
year-old boy had been ripped from a loving home and

caring family and suddenly thrust into a world of killers, rapists, and evil men who would cut their own mothers' throats without a second thought. Their only hope, nine determined men who were willing to risk everything to save them. Plus the *vaqueros* of Don Ricardo.

Keeping his eyes on the camp below, Abe said, "J.T., no matter how this thing turns out, I want to thank you for everything you've done to help."

"No need for that, Abe. We're not gonna lose this fight. We'll get those kids out of there."

Abe hesitated for a moment before he spoke again. Like John Law, he had thought of what would happen to the children if this didn't work out. If they were turned over to the Apaches. The realization that it could still happen was more than Abe Covington could bear. He couldn't allow that to happen. Turning his face toward J.T., he said, "I want you to make me a promise."

J.T. turned and looked into Abe's eyes.

"Sure, Abe. What is it?"

"That if it looks like we're gonna lose this fight an' there's no chance of gettin' them out . . . you'll . . . you'll shoot the kids."

Abe's words sent a cold chill down John Law's spine. He lowered his head and staring at the ground, replied, "I can do a lot of things, Abe, but not that. I can't shoot those two kids. You think you can?"

There were tears in the Ranger's eyes. "I'd rather see them dead than to have to suffer at the hands of the Apaches—especially Debbie. You know what they'll do to her, John. Would you want that for your niece—or any fourteen-year-old girl?"

"No, I reckon not, Abe."

"Well, when an' if the time comes, you think about

that. You think about the hours of hell that poor child will have to endure day in and day out. Just think about it, that's all. Will you do that, John? I'm gonna ask Billy and Harvey to do the same thing. If we all go down, at least they'll have a shot from up here."

"God, you're askin' an awful lot, Abe. Especially of two young fellows like Billy and Harvey. Myself, I can't promise anything. I'll have to wait and see how things work out. I'm not sayin' I won't do it."

"That's good enough for me, J.T. Thanks."

Matther crawled up next to the two men.

"Rider comin' through the pass. Just got the signal from the boys on the mountain."

"Just one man?" asked J.T.

"Looks that way."

"Keep everybody out of sight. Let him go through. Pass the word."

Matther nodded and left.

"Must be somethin' damn important for one man to go ridin' alone with those Apaches about," said Abe.

"Well, let's have a look at this fellow," said J.T., bringing the glass up to his eye.

J.T. watched the rider make his way down the mountain and to the front gates. He wore civilian clothes, but there was something about the way he sat his saddle that gave J.T. the impression he was a soldier. He didn't get a good look at the man's face until he stepped down from his horse and began talking to the guards.

"It's an American."

"Let me have a look," said Abe.

Taking the glass, Abe brought it up to his eye, then muttered. "Well, I'd be damn. You know who that is?"

"No. Do you?"

"Damn right I do. That's Major Pickett, the bastard from back at the fort that advised me against coming here. Guess we know now how the Comancheros knew about the rifles and the route the Army would be travelin'. That son of a bitch!"

Taggart joined them on the ridge. Ignoring the dirty look he received from Abe, the gunfighter said, "They said you had a rider come in. That right?"

J.T. took the glass from Abe and passed it to Taggart. "You ever seen that man before?"

Taggart looked, then lowered the glass. "Never seen him here before. Any idea who it is?"

"Major Pickett from the fort in Laredo."

Taggart nodded. "That makes sense. Purvis said he had a man on the inside that he paid for information. Mitch Lee went to see him. Guess he couldn't wait. Come for his share early."

Taggart brought the glass back up to his eye and followed the major as he rode up to the house. He expected to see Big Bill come out onto the porch, but it was Pablo Chacon who appeared instead. The major was waving his hands about and seemed to be upset about something. Chacon signaled for some men to come to the house. The major looked to be screaming at Chacon, who started laughing.

"Something ain't right down there," said Taggart.

The major turned in the saddle. Seeing four men coming toward him, he wheeled his horse and made a break for the gate. Chacon drew his pistol and fired. The major doubled over, but managed to stay in the saddle.

"He's hit. They're gonna kill him," said Taggart.

They all watched as the major tried to hold on, but any chance of escape was impossible. As he righted himself in the saddle, the men at the gates leveled their rifles and fired at the same time. Both shots struck him in the chest. Pickett tumbled backward off his horse and landed in the dirt. By now, every man with a gun was firing at the hapless soul. Pickett's body was riddled with bullets.

Taggart moved the glass back to the porch. There was no sign of Bill Purvis. Chacon walked down the steps and toward the body. It was then that Taggart saw the half-naked girl break from the house and start running for the barn. It was Debbie. Taggart thrust the glass to Abe.

"Quick—is that your niece running down there?"

Abe snatched the glass. "Debbie! My God! What have they done to her?"

He watched her race to the side of the barn. She began to claw at what looked to be a chicken cage. Then he saw young Thomas inside. She was trying to set him free. Three men ran up and grabbed her. Their hands were all over her body as she struggled to break free. It was more than Abe could stand. Dropping the glass, he pulled his gun and started to stand up as he shouted "No, goddamn you! No."

J.T. swung his leg around hard, catching the Ranger at the heels, and sent him falling backward onto the ground. Taggart grabbed for the gun in Abe's hand as he fell, and jammed the web of his thumb between the hammer and the firing pin just as the man pulled the trigger. The gun clinked. Matther and the others, having heard all the shooting, came up to the ridge.

"Grab ahold of him," shouted Taggart, "or he'll get us all killed!"

J.T. was at Abe's side. His hand went over the man's mouth.

"Now Abe, you gotta settle down. You hear me? We

only gotta wait another hour, then we're goin' down there. You start actin' crazy on us now, them kids got no chance at all. You understand what I'm sayin'?"

Abe quit struggling and nodded that he did. Seeing them put their hands on the girl, he had reacted without thinking. He quickly realized that what he had just done could have been fatal to them all. J.T. removed his hand.

"You all right now?"

Abe sat up. "Yeah. Sorry, boys. Won't happen again."

Taggart spun the gun in his hand, then rolled it over and handed it back to Abe, butt first. "We're gonna get 'em back, Ranger. You got my word on that."

As Taggart started to walk away, Abe replied, "It won't change nothin', you know?"

Taggart looked back at him. "Didn't expect it would."

As things calmed down, J.T. took Taggart and moved back into position. Pickett's body still lay where he had fallen. The man Taggart had called Chacon was slapping Debbie and pulling her back into the house. J.T. was glad he had sent Abe back with the others.

"What the hell do you make of what just went on down there?" asked John Law.

"I'm thinkin' Bill Purvis is dead and Charon has took over the outfit."

"How you figure that?"

"Chacon wouldn't dare kill a man as important as Pickett if Bill were still alive. Not without his say-so anyway. Two of 'em never did get along. The kid always thought he should be runnin' the outfit. Guess Bill finally pushed the kid too far."

"Well, at least now we know where the kids are."

Taggart agreed. As they waited, he pecked at the dirt

with a finger as he asked, "Law, you an' this Ranger close friends?"

"Yeah, I'd say so. He saved my life once during a shootout in Austin."

"You figure he'll hold to what he said earlier?"

"I'm afraid so, Frank."

"He's not fast enough, but I guess you know that?"

J.T. glanced over at Taggart. There was a sadness in his eyes. "Yeah, I know."

FOURTEEN

✶

"OKAY, BOYS. THIS is what we come for. Taggart an'
me counted close to fifty guns down there. Hard to be
sure with folks movin' from buildin' to buildin', but I'd
say that was a fair guess," said J.T. "Abe, they got Debbie
in the main house. You and Matt make that your target.
The boy's bein' kept in a cage by the wall on the south
side of the barn. Dave, your group will go for him. Me
and Taggart will try an' join you there. If we can't, don't
wait around. Once you got him, hightail it out of there.
Won't do any good to save these kids only to get 'em
killed in the middle of a shootout. So when you've got
'em, get the hell out of there. Billy and Harvey will try
to give you cover fire back up the mountain."

J.T. paused for a moment. Looking at the faces that
surrounded him, he continued. "I'd like to tell you boys

this plan we got was gonna work, but I think you all know the odds of us gettin' in there and out with no one takin' notice are pretty thin. I just want you to know I think you're all a damn good bunch of fellas an' it's been an honor ridin' with you. Now let's go."

Nine determined men, plus the brave *vaqueros,* made their way down the side of the mountain. Midway, Billy and Harvey dropped off and found themselves rifle positions that offered a full, unobstructed view of every inch of the compound. They each carried two Winchesters and two boxes of ammunition.

Farther down, Dave, Pete, and Juan and four *vaqueros* broke off and began making their way around to the west. Fifty yards on down, Abe, Matt, and four men did the same, working toward the east, while J.T. and Taggart, along with their four men, moved down to the base of the mountain and began to low-crawl toward the main gate.

The afternoon heat hung like a hot iron over their heads as Taggart nodded toward the two men at the gate. One was sitting on the ground, facing away from them with his back against the fence. The other, his rifle standing against the gate, was standing with his arms crossed over the top pole of the gate, his head down. J.T. pointed to one of the *vaqueros,* who pulled his knife and began to crawl forward. J.T. was about to point to another man when Taggart grabbed his arm and shaking his head, pulled his own knife from the sheath on his belt and began to move forward. Although John Law couldn't see the others, he knew all eyes were on the action about to take place at the main gates.

Taggart and the *vaquero* would have to cover fifteen yards of open ground in order to reach the guards. The gates were set three hundred yards from the center of the compound. This was going to be the most critical part of the job. If anyone inside happened to see what was going on at the gates and fired a shot, J.T. doubted a single one of them would ever get close to either one of the kids. But for the moment, the square was empty. Siesta time was in full swing.

Seeing the *vaquero* in position on his right, Taggart nodded, and both men stood up and slowly began walking toward the gates. Both sentries had their heads down. Moving forward softly, Taggart and the *vaquero* closed the distance between them; ten yards, seven, five, three yards. The man at the gate, still half-asleep, tipped back his sombrero and looked up. The *vaquero* leaped forward. Placing his hand behind the startled man's head, he jerked it forward, driving the knife through the man's throat. At the same instant, Taggart hurried forward, placed his hand on the forehead of the man sitting on the ground, and pulling his head back, slit the man's throat from ear to ear. As an afterthought, Taggart whistled to the *vaquero* and grabbing up the dead man's sombrero, placed it on his head. The *vaquero* did the same. They propped both dead men in a sitting position against the gate, then waved J.T. and the other *vaqueros* forward. J.T. stood up, and all four men casually strolled up to the gate and leaned against it as if they belonged there.

"Damn fine work, Frank." said J.T., his eyes darting to the left and right of the compound. "Damn fine."

"Thanks" said Taggart, nodding the same praise at the *vaquero* who had killed the other guard. "Now what?" he asked.

Out of the corner of his eye, J.T. saw Dave Matther and his bunch slipping between the rails of the corral

fence and moving toward the barn. A man carrying a saddle came out of the barn, bumping into Juan. The two
exchanged a few words before Matther stepped behind the
man, threw his hand over the man's mouth, and drove his
knife hard into the middle of his back. Catching him as
he fell, they carried him into the barn, then reappeared,
continuing to move to the north corner. The cage con-
taining the boy was midway along the south side wall. It
wouldn't take them long to get there.

"Dave's inside and almost to the cage," said J.T.

Taggart said, "Guess we ought to start moving that
way, right?"

J.T. stepped inside the gate. Leaving two *vaqueros* with
the sombreros at the gate, J.T. and the three other men
began walking toward the corral.

Meanwhile, Abe and Matt had made it to the rocks at
the rear of the house, the four *vaqueros* with them following close behind. Watching the house earlier from the
ridge, they had never seen more than three guards around
the house at any one time. There was no need to think
that had changed. Abe saw the boots of one of the guards
hanging off the east side of the porch. Spreading his men
out behind the house, Abe and Harvey moved quietly
along the east wall until they were close enough to reach
out and touch the man's boots. Abe eased his head around
the corner. The man was fast asleep. Another guard was
sleeping in a chair rocked back against the front of the
house. The third was sitting at the other end of the porch,
leaning his head against a post. Abe wasn't sure if he was
sleeping or not.

Stepping back, Abe whispered, "Two of 'em are sleep-
in', can't say about the third, but his back's to us. I'm
gonna step out and jerk this one off the porch. You're

gonna have to get your hand over his mouth before he can do any screamin'. Can you do it?"

Matt's hands were sweating, and it wasn't from the heat. "We got any choice?" he asked.

Abe shook his head from side to side. Then winked at Matt. "You'll do fine, boy. Let's get him."

Peeking around the corner again. Abe took a long step out to the side. Reaching forward with his big hands, he snatched the man by the shirt and jerked him off the porch all in one motion. Before the man could open his mouth, Matt had it covered with his hand. Turning the head to the right, Matt whipped it quickly to the left with all the strength he had. There was a crack, and the man went limp as his neck broke. Matt lowered the body to the ground. Abe stood with his knife in his hand, surprised at how easily Matt had killed the man. Winking at Abe, Matt whispered, "Let's go around and get the other bastard."

As they reached the corner of the barn, Matther saw J.T. and his men walking toward the corral. J.T. signaled that there was only one man near the cage. Matther nodded and sent Juan around the corner. He walked up on the sleeping man and sat down next to him. The man glanced over at Juan, but didn't say a word. Pulling his hat down, he went back to sleep. Seeing no one around, Juan slid his knife out and in one swift motion slit the man's throat. Easing the body down, he turned it toward the wall so no one passing by would see the blood.

Juan moved to the cage. The boy was sleeping. Removing the latch that held the cage secure, Juan knelt down and gently picked the boy up in his arms. Thomas moaned once, but then went back to sleep as he was carried to the corner of the building. As Juan joined the group again, Matther waved to J.T., who made a motion with his hand for them to get the boy out of there. Matther nodded, and they began to retrace their route back toward the corral fence.

At the house, they had disposed of the second guard. That left only the man on the porch near the front door. This one wasn't going to be as easy. There was no way anyone could walk up onto the plank porch without it making a sound. Abe called one of the *vaqueros* forward and whispered for him to go up and get the man to come around the corner. Tell him anything, but get him out of that chair and to the corner. The man nodded, and stepped around the building and up on the steps. The man in the chair looked up immediately. *"Qué pasa, amigo?"*

The *vaquero* told him the other two guards were behind the house drinking whiskey. Did he want some?

The man rocked forward, placing the legs on the chair down, and walked to the end of the porch. As he stepped around the corner, Abe drove his bowie knife deep in the man's gut and jerked it upward, carrying the body to the back of the house with the others. They all went up on the porch. Abe had the *vaqueros* take up the guards' positions while he and Matt prepared to enter the house.

There was a sudden flurry of activity coming from behind the closed door. But Abe's only thought was of Debbie and what was happening to her in that room. He started to grab the doorknob as Matt shouted, "No, Abe." As he leaped forward and pushed the Ranger away from the door, three quick gunshots tore gaping holes in the door. Two of the bullets struck Matt McMasters in the back and slammed him to the floor.

"Damnit!" said Abe. He couldn't fire back into the room because Debbie was in there. Kneeling down, he pulled Matt clear of the doorway. Blood was oozing from the man's mouth. He blinked his eyes twice as he whispered, "Go on, Abe. Save the girl. I'll—I'll be . . . all right. . . . Harvey . . . Harve . . ." A final breath left his body. Matt was dead.

Putting Matt's gun in his other hand, Abe cocked back the hammers on both guns and kicked the door in. Chacon was just going out the window when Abe fired. A bullet hit the man in the left leg as he fell out the window, crying out in pain. Sensing someone moving behind him, Abe whirled about, both guns at the ready. Debbie sat naked on the bed, her legs curled up and her tiny hands trying to hide her breasts. Tears began to stream down her face when she realized the man in the room was her uncle Abe.

Holstering his gun and pushing the other into his belt, Abe grabbed a blanket. Covering the girl, he hugged her close and whispered to her that everything was going to be all right now. They were going home. She squeezed his neck as tight as she could, the tears flowing freely as she asked about Thomas. He told her he was fine. They would be joining him soon. Grabbing her tattered dress as he went out the door, Abe carried her to the front door, then set her down. Debbie looked at Matt lying on the floor.

"Who is that?" she asked.

"A brave man that came to help save you, darlin'." Tossing her the dress, he turned his back, telling her, "Put that on, Debbie. Hurry."

The gunfire from the house had alerted the entire camp that there was trouble. J.T. and Taggart had been removing the rails to the corral when the shooting started.

"Guess the surprise is over," said Taggart, drawing his Colt.

"Damnit!" said J.T. "There'll be hell to pay now. You see Abe and the girl anywhere?"

"Yeah! He's at the front door of the main house. I think he's got the girl with him."

Comancheros began to pour out of the longhouses, their guns drawn, ready for action. J.T. looked to the west and saw Matther carrying the boy up the side of the mountain. Pete stopped and looked back when the shooting started. Rather than follow Matther and Juan, the grizzly old man headed back toward the corral. J.T. tried to wave him back, but knew that was a waste of time. Pete Simmons had said he liked a good fight, and this was shaping up to be a jim-dandy.

"Here they come!" shouted Taggart as he knelt down and fired two shots, dropping two men coming out of the long bunkhouse closest to them. J.T. drew and fired, killing another one. Two others broke to the right and tried to flank the two gunfighters, but as they charged forward, dust flew from the front of their shirts and they were knocked backward, each with a bullet hole in his chest. Billy and Harvey had dropped both men.

"Now that's what I call covering fire," said Taggart.

The entire camp now erupted into gunfire. Bullets were flying from every direction. Three Comancheros ran for the main gate, only to be cut down by Don Ricardo's *vaqueros,* who in turn were killed by a group of Chacon's men who had taken up positions near the whipping post. Others ran for the main house, and were greeted by a hail of gunfire from the *vaqueros* with Abe. J.T. kicked the last pole from the corral gate and fired his gun in the air, stampeding the animals, which now ran wild throughout the camp, causing even more confusion.

Having for the moment driven the Comancheros back

from the main house, Abe took Debbie's hand, telling her to run like she'd never run before, and they ran out the doorway, turned to the left, and ran along the porch. Bullets began ripping the wood apart behind them and above their heads. Abe knew if they hesitated at all, they were both dead. Leaping off the porch, he yelled for the *vaqueros* to follow as he led Debbie to the back of the house. But he was yelling at dead men.

Taggart and J.T. were taking a heavy toll on Chacon's men. Bodies lay all around the corral. The rifle fire from the side of the mountain was having an equally devastating effect. Taggart had looked up in time to see Abe and the girl run from the house, and told J.T. they were out and moving toward the base of the mountain. He suggested that now might be a good time for them to get the hell out of there. They had cut Chacon's force by more than half, but there were still plenty of bullets coming their way.

J.T. shook his head. "No, not just yet. We can't leave those rifles and ammunition here. Abe was right. The Apaches get their hands on that stuff, a lot of Texans are going to die. We got to blow it up."

Both men were kneeling, reloading their guns, as Taggart said, "Oh, yeah, right. An' just how the hell do you figure to do that? You carryin' some dynamite I don't know about?"

J.T. was about to answer when two bandits sprang from the corner of the barn. They had both gunfighters cold and they knew it. They grinned, but before they could pull the triggers, a deafening roar erupted and both men were slammed through the barn doors, nothing now but two bloody rag dolls shredded by Pete's shotgun. Dropping down beside J.T., the old man broke open the shotgun and pushed two more shells into the chambers.

"Brother, ya sure as hell know how to throw a party, John Law. I'll give ya that."

"Pete, we gotta blow those Army wagons. Can't let the Apaches have those guns. Any ideas?" asked Taggart.

"Yep. I'd use gunpowder."

Both men looked at him. "An' just where you gonna get that?" asked J.T.

Pete nodded toward the barn. "Right there."

Taggart and J.T. looked in the barn. The blast from Pete's shotgun had driven the men through the doors. Next to their ripped and torn bodies sat three kegs of black powder. Without a word being said, Taggart ran into the barn, grabbed two kegs, and with one under each arm, went out the back of the barn and around to the ammunition wagons. From the hillside, Dave, Juan, and Abe had joined in with their rifles and were doing a good job of keeping the remaining Comancheros pinned down. Every now and then, one would try to make a move and be cut down by three or four bullets. That quickly discouraged others from making the same mistake.

Pete crouched down and began to move toward the barn.

"Where you goin', Pete?" asked J.T.

"He's gonna need some help with that powder. We get her set, we'll be back."

Bullets splintered the wood around the barn doors as Pete ran through to the other side and headed for the wagons. Taggart was nowhere in sight. Pete ran up to the first wagon and looked inside. It was filled with rifles. When he turned around, he felt a burning pain rip through his stomach as he came face-to-face with a breed. The man had a grin on his face. Each time he pushed the knife deeper, his grin got wider.

"Ooooh, damn!" said Pete as he felt himself slipping away. He tried to raise the scattergun, but it seemed to weigh a ton now. The breed knocked the gun away and as Pete was falling, Dog caught him. Pushing the old man back against the wagon, he jerked the knife from Pete's stomach and cut off his left ear. Stepping back and holding his trophy high in the air, he watched Pete fall to the ground. Bringing the ear down, Dog ran his fingers back and forth over it. It was too rough and old. He tossed it away.

Shoving a barrel of the gunpowder into the center of the cases of ammunition, Taggart fashioned a fuse from a piece of rope and put it in place. Backing out of the wagon, he didn't see Dog standing behind the wagon with his knife raised and ready to drive it into his back. As Taggart's feet touched the ground, he heard Pete's voice yell, "Taggart—drop!"

The gunfighter went straight to the ground just as a shotgun blast ripped over his head. Taggart felt something warm and runny on his hands and along the left side of his face. It was blood. When he looked, he saw Pete standing over him. Blood poured from the side of his head. His pants were covered in blood. Before Taggart could get to his feet, the old man fell in front of him.

"Ya boys throw a hell of a fine . . . party. . . ."

Taggart reached over and closed the old outlaw's eyes. He was gone.

Out of the corner of his eye, Taggart saw someone come around the wagon. With lightning-quick speed, he drew his gun and turned. It was John Law. He looked down at Pete. He sighed when he saw the old man's ear was missing.

"He's gone. Dog got him," said Taggart. "He's layin' back there—or what's left of him anyway. First time I had my life saved by a dead man."

Turning away from the old man he'd grown fond of, J.T. asked, "How's the powder comin'?"

"One's ready. Other one'll take a few minutes."

"Get it done. I'll cover you."

Taggart crawled into the second ammunition wagon. A few minutes later, he backed out, holding a thin piece of rope. He knotted it together with the rope from the first wagon. Seeing a kerosene lamp hanging on the side of the rig, he grabbed it, unscrewed the cap, and poured a line of the liquid along each piece of rope. When he was finished, he took a match from his vest pocket. "You call it."

"Light it up an' let's get the hell outta here."

Taggart struck the match and touched it to the kerosene-soaked rope. A flame leaped up and began running along the length of the rope. The two men broke for the back of the barn and headed for the rocks twenty yards beyond. They made it just as the wagons exploded in a cloud of black and gray smoke that sent pieces of wagon, gun cases, and exploding ammunition raining down all over the camp.

"Maybe we should have brought Pete's body out of there?" said Taggart.

J.T. shook his head. "No, that old bastard would've wanted to go out with a bang."

Taggart managed a grin. "Guess you're right about that."

"Let's get back with the others and see how those kids are doin'," said J.T.

The massive explosion had taken all the fight out of the remaining Comancheros. If John Law and his bunch were leaving, they were willing to leave well enough alone. Their camp was a shambles. Dead men lay everywhere. Crying women and children began to come out from their hiding places, and were in awe of the amount of destruction that had been rained down on them.

At the top of the ridge, J.T. found Abe and the children surrounded by the rest of the group. They moved aside as Taggart and J.T. came up. Both kids were clinging to Abe, almost afraid to let go for fear that they might wake up and find this was all a dream. Debbie looked battered and bruised, and J.T. could tell by the look in Abe's eyes that she had been raped. As bad as that was, at least they were still alive. Considering the odds they had just faced, that was a miracle in itself. Young Thomas, his face covered with dirt, looked up at Taggart and John Law and, tears streaking down his cheeks, in his child's voice said, "Thank you for coming to help us."

It was enough to make the hardest among them tear up a bit. It was then that J.T. saw Matt was missing. He looked over at Harvey. The big man's eyes showed that he wanted to cry, but he stood rock-solid, trying to fight back the pain of the loss. His brother would have wanted it that way.

"Where's Pete?" asked Billy.

Taggart dropped his head and kicked at the dirt with the toe of his boot as he said, "He didn't make it."

Looking at Dave Matther, J.T. asked, "How bad did Don Ricardo's men get hurt?"

"Five dead, three wounded," came the reply.

Turning to Abe next, Law asked, "The kids doin' well enough to travel?"

Abe nodded. "They'll be fine, John T."

"Well, I think we stung 'em pretty bad down there, and with their horses scattered all over the place, I don't think they're in any hurry to come chasin' after us. But we better get moving anyway. Taggart, you take the point."

Taggart began backing away from the group as he replied, "Don't think so this time, J.T. You boys go on without me. Pablo Chacon's still alive and hidin' down there somewhere. Saw him limpin' from the house after he fell out of the window. Kinda lost track of him after that. But he'll try to get outta there sometime, an' I plan to be waitin' for him when he does. This won't be over till he's dead. I owe that little girl that much."

"He might not be comin' outta there alone, Frank," said J.T.

"He'll be the first one to go down. Doesn't really matter much after that."

Abe passed the kids over to Juan and stood up.

"You forgettin' we got business?" asked Abe.

Frank's hand moved down and a little behind his holster. He didn't want to draw on the Ranger, especially with the kids right there, but he wasn't going to stand still and get himself shot with a fight.

"Nope. I ain't forgot, Ranger. It's your game. You start dealin' anytime you're ready."

"Let it go, Abe," said J.T. "This man's done more than keep his word to us."

Some of the others agreed and said so, but Abe seemed set on pushing it to the end. Debbie began to understand what was about to happen, and began to scream for her uncle not to do this. But even that didn't seem to help.

"Goddamnit, Abe, you're not fast enough to take him. Don't you understand that?" said J.T. "He's a professional, Abe. He don't wanta shoot you. Can't you see that? Let it go, damnit. You got the kids back—that's what you wanted, isn't it? What's gonna happen to them if you're dead? Have you thought about that? Hell, no, you haven't. All that matters to Abe Covington is that he get his damn revenge. To hell with everything and everybody else. Aw, hell with it. Go ahead an' shoot the dumb son of a bitch, Frank. So we can get the hell outta here."

J.T. walked away. The others began to move back. Juan tried to take the children down the trail, but Debbie refused to go. Instead, she cried out, "Please, Uncle Abe. Don't do this. Mama wouldn't want you to. Please, Uncle Abe, we don't have anyone else. Don't you leave us too."

"Aw, hell!" said Taggart. The gunfighter drew and fired his gun so fast that it was all over before anyone saw it come out of the holster.

Abe yelled and grabbed his gun hand. Debbie broke away from Juan and ran to her uncle, with Thomas right behind her. Tearing a piece of her dress off, she took the Ranger's hand and gently began to wrap it. Angry that her uncle had been hurt, Debbie looked at Taggart.

"You're a bad man, Mr. Taggart."

Taggart could barely hold back a smile. "Yes, ma'am, I reckon I am at that."

Abe was still furious. "This don't end it, Taggart."

"No, sir, didn't think it would. But when you got that hand healed up and that young lady there married off to a proper gentleman, then taught the boy how to run his daddy's ranch, you come on out to Arizona and we'll talk about it again."

Frank Taggart's words brought a smile to everyone

there except Abe. But he'd get over it. Abe didn't realize it yet, but Frank Taggart was a lot smarter than people realized. With one shot he had avoided a deadly confrontation, and with a few well-chosen words had just given Abe Covington a view of the wonderful life that lay ahead of him.

As they helped Abe to his horse and prepared to leave, J.T. walked over to Taggart. "Thanks."

"For what?"

"For not killin' him."

Taggart smiled. "Well, won't do much for my reputation, that's for sure."

J.T. smiled for a moment, then turned serious. "You want me to stay behind to help you out here?"

Taggart shook his head. "Naw, that's okay, J.T. But I'm obligated. This is something I've got to do alone. Figure it's the only way I can redeem myself for what happened. When Chacon's dead, it'll be finished. You have my word on that."

Reaching out his hand, J.T. said, "Been a pleasure workin' with you, Frank. Maybe our trails will cross again someday."

Taggart took the bounty man's hand in a firm grip as he said, "You never can tell. Adios, John Law."

As Juan led the group out of the arroyo at the base of the Chomais Pass, they heard gunfire echoing through the canyons. They stopped and turned to look back. The sound was a mix of rifle fire and pistol shots. It only lasted three or four minutes; then the canyon walls were silent again. J.T. waved Juan on. If they hurried, they could make it to Don Ricardo's hacienda before dark.

Soon, they were out on the open plain. As the group moved ahead, J.T. paused for a moment and looked back at the mountains. He could hear the laughter of Matt McMasters, the swaggering bravado of Shotgun Pete, and the final words of Frank Taggart.

Had those shots signaled the end of this affair as Taggart had wanted? J.T. knew he might never know the answer to that question. But as he turned and straightened himself in the saddle, there was one thing he did know— Frank Taggart was a man of his word.

J. R. ROBERTS
THE GUNSMITH